"Run!"

Dominic wasn't sure he could stand, much less run, but he staggered after her, letting her pull him behind her. They pushed farther into the trees seconds before another bullet whipped past his head and buried itself into the thick trunk of the tree he'd just ducked behind.

"Who's shooting at you?" she asked, huddling next to him.

"I think it's the fugitive we were chasing."

"How'd he get away from you? How'd he get a gun?"

"We didn't have him. That's why we were going after him. To take him into custody. He saw us and bolted." He paused. "He must have doubled back to get behind us. And I don't know where the gun came from."

Another shot pinged off the ground two feet away, and Katherine flinched. "Don't we need to find a way out of here?"

"He can't hit us from the angle he's shooting from. Might come close, but..."

"What if he changes angles?"

"Then we'll have a problem."

Lynette Eason is a bestselling, award-winning author who makes her home in South Carolina with her husband and two teenage children. She enjoys traveling, spending time with her family and teaching at various writing conferences around the country. She is a member of Romance Writers of America and American Christian Fiction Writers. Lynette can often be found online interacting with her readers. You can find her on Facebook.com/lynette.eason and on Twitter, @lynetteeason.

Books by Lynette Eason

Love Inspired Suspense

Holiday Homecoming Secrets
Peril on the Ranch
Mountain Fugitive

True Blue K-9 Unit

Justice Mission

Wrangler's Corner

The Lawman Returns
Rodeo Rescuer
Protecting Her Daughter
Classified Christmas Mission
Christmas Ranch Rescue
Vanished in the Night
Holiday Amnesia

Military K-9 Unit

Explosive Force

Classified K-9 Unit

Bounty Hunter

Visit the Author Profile page at Harlequin.com for more titles.

MOUNTAIN FUGITIVE

LYNETTE EASON

LOVE INSPIRED SUSPENSE
INSPIRATIONAL ROMANCE

LOVE INSPIRED® SUSPENSE
INSPIRATIONAL ROMANCE

Recycling programs
for this product may
not exist in your area.

ISBN-13: 978-1-335-55456-7

Mountain Fugitive

Copyright © 2021 by Lynette Eason

This edition published by arrangement with Harlequin Books S.A.

For questions and comments about the quality of this book, please contact us
at CustomerService@Harlequin.com.

Love Inspired
22 Adelaide St. West, 40th Floor
Toronto, Ontario M5H 4E3, Canada
www.Harlequin.com

Printed in U.S.A.

I will lift up mine eyes unto the hills,
from whence cometh my help.
—*Psalm* 121:1

Dedicated to the Savior.

ONE

When the gunshot rang out, Dr. Katherine Gilroy pulled her horse to a stop and waited for her friend Isabelle McGee to catch up. "What do you think that's all about?" Katherine asked.

Isabelle and her husband, Mac, owned the property that stretched for acres—as well as the horse named Hotshot now stomping the ground. He hated loud noises. Katherine didn't blame him.

"No idea," Isabelle said. "Maybe Cody Ray came across a rattler or something—but I really doubt that, since he didn't say anything about working in this area today."

Cody Ray was one of the hands for the ranch and was often out on the land checking fences or moving cattle. But this was a Saturday morning, and Katherine knew Cody Ray usually saved those chores for the workweek.

Two more quick shots raised Isabelle's brows.

Katherine frowned. "That sounds more like an *or something* than a rattler."

"And Cody Ray wouldn't need more than one bullet to take care of a snake—or any other wild animal."

Hotshot pranced and stomped his back feet. Katherine tightened her knees then kicked her heels against his side to get him moving again. Isabelle's paint fell into step beside her. "It's kind of hard to tell," Katherine said, "but I think it came from behind those trees. Someone might be in trouble and signaling for help."

"Of course this would happen while Mac's out of town," Isabelle muttered with a frown. Mac had taken several horses to an auction in Tryon, North Carolina, and wouldn't be back until late the next day. Isabelle rubbed her nose. "What do you think? Should I call 911?"

"Why don't we see what's going on first?"

"Okay."

Katherine guided her horse in the direction of the shots. Maybe riding toward them was stupid, but if someone needed help, she had the training to offer it.

They followed the path to the ridge where the trees thickened and the underbrush did its best to obscure the way. Hotshot continued his restless dance, shaking his head and making Katherine work to keep her seat. She was an experienced horsewoman and Hotshot needed the exercise, but if someone continued shooting, keeping control of the animal was going to require all her skill.

She led the way, her heart pounding a little faster, mentally reviewing the steps she'd take to treat a gunshot wound with the limited supplies she carried in the saddlebag. A first-aid kit with bandages, snakebite antivenin, a tourniquet, pain meds and antibiotic ointment. Not the ideal situation, but she could work with it.

They crested the hill and stopped just as the white sky released the first few snowflakes of the season.

Isabelle pointed. "There, by the tree line. Two people on the ground."

"Call for help," Katherine said, "I'll see if they're still alive."

Isabelle gaped. "There's a shooter out there."

"I know. And your kids are at the house alone. Go. Hurry." Isabelle and Mac had a house full of kids—two new foster children and three of their own they'd adopted last year. The oldest was sixteen. Fully capable of caring for the younger ones on a normal day. A shooter on the property changed everything.

Katherine could tell Isabelle wanted to offer more protests, but if the men had been shot, they might still be alive. And in the case of gunshot wounds, quick action was often the difference between life and death.

"You're a doctor, Katherine," Isabelle said, "not a soldier or a cop."

But, as a former tactical medic, she had the training to take care of this and they both new it. Katherine had worked closely with a SWAT team, providing medical care when necessary. She'd saved many lives that hadn't been able to wait on traditional EMS. Katherine narrowed her eyes while Isabelle bit her lip and pulled out her phone.

She dialed 911, but said to Katherine, "I'll call Cody Ray and ask him to—no, I forgot, he's in town and Ms. Sybil is with him. Zoe took Sadie to the doctor for a checkup. So, whoever's shooting isn't anyone connected to the ranch." Ms. Sybil was cook, housekeeper and part-time babysitter rolled into one. Zoe was a former foster child turned single mother living with Isabelle and Mac while she figured out her next steps in life.

"Which means you need to go back there and be with

the kids," Katherine said. "I'll be fine." She held still and listened for a fraction longer. "I don't hear any more shots. Whoever was shooting probably thinks his job is done and hightailed it out of here." Hopefully. "But just to be on the safe side, you need to go now."

"I can tell by the look on your face you're going to go check on them."

"Just like you would do if you didn't have kids at the house."

"I know. Just be careful, and I'll let Creed and the others know they need to get a move on."

"Of course." Katherine kicked Hotshot into a trot, then a full gallop, as she headed for the men, praying she could do something to help them. She wasn't nearly as confident as she'd conveyed to Isabelle, but she couldn't let those men bleed out if she could do something about it. "Please, God, don't let me get shot," she muttered, "and please let them be alive." Flashbacks from her paramedic days tickled the edges of her mind and it was all she could do to keep the memories at bay.

The shots had come from her right, so she leaned against the left side of the horse's mane, trying to make herself as small a target as possible. The men had been ambushed and lay next to the tree line. She guessed they'd started running for cover at the first shot. One was about six feet ahead of the other, more under the cover of the trees.

Heart pounding a rapid beat, Katherine pulled Hotshot to a stop between the men and the direction the bullets had come from, praying the person wouldn't shoot the horse. She slid from the saddle, leaving the reins trailing the ground, then snagged the first-aid kit from the saddlebag. US marshals according to the vests the men wore.

Looked like their prisoner or fugitive had turned the tables on them. Which meant the person was either gone now that he'd taken care of the threat—or she was now a target because she planned to try to help the men. A quick scan of the area didn't reveal anything unusual or worrisome, but the trees could easily be hiding the sniper.

Still using the horse as a shield, she hurried to the man closest to her. The bullet had hit him just above his left ear and he'd landed on his side. His brown, sightless eyes stared up at her and she knew he was beyond help. She checked his pulse anyway and got what she expected. Nothing.

She closed the dead man's eyes then turned her attention to the other one. A pulse. She focused on his head. A gash just below his hairline bled freely. A low groan rumbled from him and Katherine placed a hand on his shoulder. "Don't move," she said.

He blinked and she caught a glimpse of sapphire-blue eyes. He let out another groan. "Carl…"

"Just stay still and let me look at your head."

"I'm fine." He rolled to his side and he squinted up at her. "Who're you?"

"I'm Dr. Katherine Gilroy so I think I'm the better judge of whether or not you're fine. You have a head wound which means possible concussion." She reached for him. "What's your name?"

He pushed her hand away. "Dominic O'Ryan. A branch caught me. Knocked me loopy for a few seconds, but not out. We were running from the shooter." His eyes sharpened. "He's still out there." His hand went to his right hip, gripping the empty holster next to the badge on his belt. A star within a circle. "Where's my gun? Where's Carl? My partner, Carl Manning. We need to get out of here."

"I'm sorry," Katherine said, her voice soft. "He didn't make it."

He froze. Then horror sent his eyes wide—and searching. They found the man behind her and Dominic shuddered. "No. No, no, no. Carl! Carl!" He army crawled to his partner and sucked in a gasping breath, cupped Carl's face and felt for a pulse.

Katherine didn't bother to tell him she'd already done the same—or what he'd find. After a few seconds, he let out a low cry then sucked in another deep breath and composed his features. The intense moment has lasted only a few seconds, but Katherine knew he was compartmentalizing, stuffing his emotions into a place he could hold them and deal with them later.

She knew because she'd often done the same thing. Still did on occasion.

In spite of that, his grief was palpable, and Katherine's heart thudded with sympathy for him. She moved back to give him some privacy, her eyes sweeping the hills around them once more. Again, she saw nothing, but the hairs on the back of her neck were standing straight up. Hotshot had done well, standing still, being a buffer between them and a possible sniper, but Katherine's nerves were twitching—much like when she'd worked with the police department. "I think we need to find some better cover."

As if to prove her point, another crack sounded, and Hotshot reared. His whinnying scream echoed around them. Then he bolted for home. Katherine grabbed the first-aid kit with one hand and pulled Dominic to his feet with the other. "Run!"

Dominic wasn't sure he could stand, much less run, but he staggered after her, letting her pull him behind her. They pushed farther into the trees seconds before another bullet whipped past his head and buried itself into the thick trunk of the tree he'd just ducked behind.

"Who's shooting at you?" she asked, huddling next to him.

"I think it's the fugitive we were chasing."

"How'd he get away from you? How'd he get a gun?"

"We didn't have him. That's why we were going after him. To take him into custody. He saw us and bolted." He paused. "He must have doubled back to get behind us. And I don't know where the gun came from."

He studied the woman who'd braved gunfire to help him. She was tall, probably about four inches shorter than his own six feet two inches, and had her dark blond hair pulled into a messy ponytail. Strands had escaped to frame her tanned face and intelligent dark brown eyes blinked up at him. Being this close to her, he inhaled the scent of horses and the outdoors with each breath. He liked it and realized it was a smell that fit her. She was pretty in a way that definitely caught his attention, but more wholesome girl next door rather than magazine model.

Another shot pinged off the ground two feet away and Katherine flinched. "Don't we need to find a way out of here?"

"He can't hit us from the angle he's shooting from. Might come close, but…"

"What if he changes angles?"

"Then we'll have a problem." He paused. "I think I'm going to be sick." He closed his eyes and swallowed, praying the nausea would fade. He never liked being sick, but losing his breakfast in front of this woman would be humiliating. Of course, that was the least of his worries. *I'm sorry, Carl...*

"You probably have a slight concussion," she said. "How's your vision?"

"Fine." A bit wobbly, but it would be fine. He didn't have a choice. Dominic glanced around the side of the large trunk, saw nothing and pulled back, fighting another wave of sickness. "How come you're so calm and cool while getting shot at?" he asked, trying to ignore the twisting sensation in his gut. Most everyone outside of law enforcement or military would be freaking out. And it had nothing to do with her gender. He was including men in that generalization.

"I was a tactical medic in Atlanta, Georgia, for four years."

"That's a story I'd like to hear, but for now, we need help."

"Isabelle, my friend who was with me when we heard the shots, called the police, but it'll take some time for them to get out here."

Time they didn't have.

"So, we're on our own for a bit." It wasn't a question. "Yes."

"Where's my phone?" he muttered. He patted his cargo pants and finally found the device in the side pocket. No signal. Great. A flash of movement in the trees sent alarm crashing through him. "Okay, shooter's changing angles. We're going to need a better hiding place." If he could move. The doctor was eyeing him like she was wondering the same thing. "I'll make it," he assured her.

"Then come on. Hold on to me if you need to."

Determined not to need to, Dominic, nevertheless, grabbed her hand this time and headed for a thicker area of trees. The undergrowth slowed them down and he could only pray it was doing the same for the shooter.

A hard yank on his arm pulled him to a stumbling stop. "What is it?"

"There." She pointed. "Can you go up some? There's a small cave behind those trees. It's not perfect, but it'll provide some coverage."

He followed her pointing finger to the area that would hide them well if he could manage to get up there. "Go. I'm right behind you."

She shot him a worried look but did as he ordered and scrambled up the side of the hill to the opening. She slipped inside and he followed with a grunt.

The chill of the sheltered space made him shiver while the pain in his head shot down the back of his neck and into his shoulders. He gripped his weapon in his right hand and stood at the entrance, watching. Waiting. At least no one could sneak up behind them.

Nothing moved. "I've lost track of him," he said in a low whisper. He pulled his phone from his pocket. "And I've still got no signal."

"It's spotty in this area," she answered, her voice as low as his. "But Isabelle's sending help."

Which he appreciated, but even if help arrived in the next five minutes, that was probably going to be too late.

TWO

Katherine wanted to pace. Instead, she watched the man who'd survived a murder attempt and wondered how long it would be before he crashed. Adrenaline would keep him on his feet for only so long.

His shoulders were broad and strong, and he looked like he could handle just about any trouble that life threw at him—but, as she well knew, bullets could take down the strongest of men.

Katherine stepped next to him. "Anything?"

He shook his head then gasped and pressed a palm to his temple. She placed a hand on his elbow. "Please, let me look at you."

He sighed. "Fine."

She pulled out her phone and turned on the flashlight app. "Look at me."

He did and her breath caught. His eyes were *really* blue. And his lashes were *really* long. And it was *really* unfair that a man would have eyes that pretty.

She cleared her throat and snapped the light into his eyes. "Pupils are even so that's good." He blinked. "But if you're still feeling nauseous, that might indicate a slight concussion. You need to rest and take it easy for the next twenty-four to forty-eight hours." She paused. "Assuming we get out of here alive and to the point of you being able to do that."

"Yeah. Let's focus on that first."

She shot him a tight smile and stepped back. His gaze lingered on hers for a split second before he turned back to the opening and looked out. "How far is your place from here?"

"I live in town above the medical clinic. My car is back at Isabelle's house which is about half a mile south of here." She frowned. "But it's a lot of wide-open pasture. We'd be sitting ducks if we tried to walk it."

He sighed and rubbed his eyes. "Great. And my vehicle is back on the road. The guy we were chasing crashed his stolen truck into a tree, climbed out and took off through the woods. We followed him, but somehow, he must have gotten behind us and…ah, I don't know. I can't think." She didn't like the lack of color in his face.

"Like I said, a slight concussion. Foggy thinking is one of the symptoms."

He scowled.

A sound from outside their little hiding place stiffened his shoulders and he went still. Katherine did, too, her nerves stretching.

Then all was silent.

Dominic raised a finger to his lips, and she nodded.

Another sound reached her, and relief swirled when she recognized the sound of helicopter blades beating the chilly morning air and sirens wailing in the distance. "Help is almost here," she whispered.

"Yeah, now we just have to let them know where we are without alerting the shooter."

"You don't think all of the cops will be enough to scare him off?"

"Depends on how bad he wants to put a bullet in me."

If his partner was anything to go by, that was pretty bad. She shuddered. "I have a hand flare in the first-aid kit, but it'll alert the shooter, too. Could stick it in the ground, light it and hightail it away from that area and wait for the police to come to us."

He hesitated. "All right. Give it me. I'll do it."

"Actually, I was thinking I would. You have a concussion and might pass out before you actually get it planted or lit."

"You said a mild concussion, and I can handle it."

"You're stubborn."

"Very." He paused. "I get the feeling you are, too."

"Very." She pulled the flare out of the bag and walked toward him. He held out a hand and she bypassed him to step through the opening.

"Katherine—"

She turned to look him in the eye. "I don't have a head injury, and I don't have a sniper after me. Please don't argue with me about this."

He wavered. Before he could protest further, she slipped outside and started to climb, looking for an open area she could place the flare. A modern-day smoke signal. Thankfully, it had rained just before dawn and the ground was still wet and soft enough to dig a hole. She shoved the end of the flare into the soil.

When no gunshots came her way, she breathed a little easier, but knew she wasn't in the clear yet. She quickly removed the cap of the flare and scraped it against the black button. With a hiss, the flame came to life and smoke billowed from it.

Katherine bolted back to the hiding place and slipped inside the opening to find Dominic on the floor, eyes squinting against the pain. His head must feel like it had been cracked open. She hurried to his side, checked his eyes and took his pulse. Steady, but fast. "I'm fine," he said.

"Well, if we can ever get out of here, you will be."

"Tactical medic, huh?"

"Yep. It was an interesting time in my life."

"I'm sure."

"Katherine!"

Isabelle's voice.

Katherine went to the opening and looked out. Relief and gratitude swept her when she saw her friend leading the officers toward the flare. Officers that included Sheriff Creed Payne and Deputy Ben Land—both good friends of Katherine. Their vehicles were parked at the base of the hill along with two ambulances.

"We're in here!" She waved and Creed changed course to head toward their little hideout.

She turned back to Dominic. "Backup is here. I think the sniper is probably long gone by now. Do you think you can walk down to the ambulance or should we get that chopper to lower a basket for you?"

He shot her a baleful look. "I'll walk, thanks."

"Then I'll go in front of you and catch you when you pass out."

He huffed a short laugh and pushed himself off the wall. "I've never been one to back down from a challenge." He sobered, his eyes turning bleak. "I have to see to Carl before I go anywhere."

"The medical examiner is here. I saw her van. She'll take care of Carl."

"You have an ME in a town this small?"

"We're small, but we're mighty." She gave him a sympathetic smile. "We have a forty-five bed hospital, too, believe it or not. There's a morgue in the basement and that's where they'll take your partner. The ME works there part-time. I never can keep up with what her schedule is, but to get here that fast, she must have been at the hospital when the call came in."

He nodded, then winced at the movement. "Gotta stop doing that for a while."

"Good idea." She slid an arm around his waist. "Come on—you can lean on me. I'm stronger than I look."

He hesitated as though trying to decide if he would take her up on her offer. "I'm not used to leaning on people," he finally said, his voice low.

She blinked and offered him a small smile. "Well, join the club. But for now, I'm your best hope of not falling on your face in front of anyone else."

His arm came up to rest on her shoulders. "Right. We wouldn't want that."

"Then you can rest and heal, then get back to chasing your fugitive." And grieving the loss of his partner. Her heart pounded as she led him out of their little hideaway to meet the paramedics halfway. Creed was with them and Katherine made the introductions. "Dominic, this is Creed Payne, the sheriff. Sheriff, meet Dominic O'Ryan."

The two men shook hands.

"Did you see our car at the edge of the woods?" Dominic asked Creed.

"I have a deputy who found it, yeah. I instructed him to have the towing company take it to the office. Keys weren't in it."

"Check Carl's pocket." A muscle jumped in Dominic's jaw and Katherine wanted to place soothing fingers on it. She often wished she could do more for her patients, but this man was different. She wanted to take all of his pain away, hold him and let him grieve. She cleared her throat and looked at her phone to distract herself. Then shoved it in her pocket when she realized what she was doing. There was no signal so nothing new on there she needed to see.

"Will do," Creed said. "Found the wrecked truck, too. Having it towed, as well. Plates came back stolen."

"Yeah, our guy managed to grab a vehicle with the keys in it." He sighed. "Would it be possible for you to get the go bag and the laptop from my car and bring it to the hospital for me? I don't want to leave it there."

"Of course."

"Thanks." He looked at Katherine. "Looks like I'm ready."

Once he was in the back of the ambulance, she climbed in with him. "Will you let me give you a more thorough examination now?"

"Since I think I'm about to pass out, now might be a good time."

Awareness came like a punch in the gut. Dominic blinked open his eyes and found himself staring at fluorescent lights. He knew he was in the hospital simply because of the smells and sounds that hit him.

Memories returned and grief slammed him, and he rolled to his side to curl his fingers around the pillow. Carl was dead. Not just his partner, but one of his best friends for the past five years.

"Dominic?"

The soft voice intruded, and he wanted to yell at her to go away. Instead, he sucked in a breath and twisted back to see the woman who'd braved bullets to help him standing just inside the door. She gave him a soft smile. "Hi."

"Hi." His voice came out husky. Hoarse. He cleared his throat.

"So, how's the head?"

"Not too bad." He was happy to realize that was the truth.

"I put in three stitches and prescribed some pain-killers. You can pick them up at the pharmacy on your way out."

"Thank you. Have you heard if the crime-scene unit found anything?"

"Bullet casings and footprints, but other than that, I'm not sure. Deputy Ben Land retrieved the items from your car that you asked for." She motioned to the chair in the corner and he noted the bags. She stepped closer and checked the IV machine. "The medical examiner has Carl's personal effects ready for you to pick up whenever you or his family can get them."

"I don't know how I'm going to tell his parents. They're going to be devastated." He closed his eyes at the mental picture and wanted to weep.

"Cindy—the ME—has already called them. They're on the way."

"Oh." He started to nod and thought better of it. "Thank you." He paused. "How long have I been out?"

"About four hours."

"Four hours!" He started to sit up. When the room tilted, he quickly settled back down with a groan. "Great. I'm assuming my fugitive escaped."

"I would assume. Everything around the area is on lockdown. I haven't had a chance to catch the news yet as I've been checking on other patients here in the hospital, but I haven't heard otherwise."

He picked up the remote from the bedside table and aimed it at the television. The screen flickered to life and he scrolled until he came to the national news channel. Nothing there. "What's the local news channel?"

"Seven."

He switched to that and Katherine recognized the news anchor. "…the fugitive who still hasn't been named is on the run and was last seen in Timber Creek, North Carolina. He is said to be armed and dangerous and desperate. Authorities are asking everyone to lock your doors and to please, please, do not confront this individual in any way. Dial 911 if you see anyone suspicious. We hope to have a photo of this person, who has killed one US marshal and wounded another, soon. Thank you. Steve?"

Dominic shut off the television and groaned. "He didn't wound me. I ran into a tree branch when I looked back to see where Carl was."

"Does it matter?"

"Yes. Facts matter. Details matter. He might be a fugitive, but I'm not blaming him for something he didn't do." He pressed the palm of his hand to his forehead. "He killed Carl. I'll blame him for that."

And that just gave her quite a bit of insight into his character. Interesting. "Where are you from?"

"Asheville."

"Oh, not too far from here."

"A little over an hour." He'd stated the obvious and

flushed. Of course, she knew how far Asheville was from her little town, but he wanted to keep her talking.

She nodded. "So, what did this fugitive do?"

"He's a witness for the prosecution in an upcoming trial. We were protecting him, and he took off." He pressed his palm to his temple. "He's just a kid and before today, I would have said he wasn't violent. But as soon as the people he was going to testify against see the news, they're going to come after him, too, and he's going to wind up dead. And a very bad person is going to walk away from the justice he deserves."

"Then I guess the marshals and other law enforcement better find him first."

"Exactly."

She tilted her head and studied him. "Why would he run from those who were protecting him? That doesn't make sense."

Dominic's jaw tightened. "When we catch him, that's the first question I plan to ask him."

"He didn't give you any indication that he'd planned to run?"

"None."

"Or that he wanted to kill you?"

He sighed. "No, like I said, I never would have thought he had it in him." He paused. "We had two incidents that might have scared him into running, but I thought we had him convinced everything would be all right from here on out. That we had it under control." He shrugged. "I see now I was mistaken. Then again, I didn't think he had a violent bone in his body. Guess my ability to make sound judgments about people is way off because I sure didn't see this coming."

Katherine blew out a low sigh. "All right, so what's your plan for when you leave here?"

"First, I need to check in with my director and fill him in, although, he probably already knows about the chase. Two other agents were about twenty minutes behind Carl and me. They would have filled him in. But I doubt they know about Carl yet."

"That's probably who's been blowing up your phone." She handed it to him, and he noticed the number of missed calls.

"Thanks." He checked the number. "Yeah, that's my director."

"He must have sent some of your fellow marshals, too. There are two of them in the waiting room demanding answers. Do you mind if I fill them in?"

"No, thanks. I'll do it." He sat up. Slowly. When the room stayed right side up, he turned and planted his feet on the floor. Katherine moved closer, hands out as though to catch him if necessary. He really hoped it wouldn't be. "Okay," he said, "I'm ready to get out of here."

"Dominic?"

"Yes?"

"You have a slight concussion. You need to rest. You can't go chasing this guy in your condition."

"Which means you're off this case until you heal up," a voice said from the door. Dominic recognized that voice and gave a mental groan. "Hi, Beth." The woman who was just as tall as Katherine stepped into the room. A man followed her. "Owen."

"Sorry to intrude," Beth said, "but I've been asked for an update."

Dominic scowled. "Beth Wilson, Owen Charles, this

is Dr. Katherine Gilroy. Katherine, meet two of my fellow marshals, Beth and Owen." He narrowed his eyes. "And I'm fine."

"You don't look it," Beth said. "And that's what I'm going to tell the director."

"I'm not leaving here without that witness," Dominic said, his voice low. "He killed Carl."

Grief flashed in Beth's eyes, and it comforted Dominic to know she felt the same as he did and would do everything in her power to make sure Noah Bennett didn't go free.

"Look," Katherine said, "I have an idea." All eyes turned on her. She nodded to Dominic. "You need someone to keep an eye on you through the night. You don't really need to stay in the hospital, but I wouldn't want you driving home, either." She narrowed her eyes. "You just said you wouldn't go anyway."

She was right. "I'll get a hotel," he said. "I'm here until this guy is back in custody."

"Hear me out on my idea. I'm off tomorrow and the next three days. You can stay with me tonight and we'll see how you are in the morning. If you don't have any issues for the next forty-eight hours, I'll consider clearing you."

Beth nodded. "The boss will go for that." She glanced at Owen. "Don't you think?"

"Yeah. Sure. I can't see why not."

Dominic started to argue, but stopped. He felt lousy. He wasn't the only good agent on the case, and he needed to listen to reason. He didn't like it, of course, but he wasn't stupid. "Fine." He was getting really tired of that word.

Beth and the doctor exchanged a glance. If it had

been a smug look, he'd have balked, but it was sheer relief that he'd agreed and they didn't have to argue with him anymore.

An hour later, after a stop at the general store where he barely made it through the purchasing of two changes of clothes and some toiletries, he collapsed back into the passenger seat of her Jeep. "I could have done that for you," she said.

"I know, but I'm picky about stuff."

"Shocker."

"Ha." He must have dozed because the next thing he knew she was parked behind a building and he had no memory of getting there.

"We're here," she said.

"I see that." He climbed out of the vehicle and held on for a few seconds while he waited for the ground to stop rocking. A low growl to his left snapped his head up. He ignored the sharp stabbing pain and focused on a very large German shepherd walking toward them. "Katherine?"

"I see him. That's Buddy. He used to belong to Mr. White who worked in search and rescue for a while. Before Mr. White died from cancer six months ago, he would bring Buddy to his appointments so Buddy's familiar with the clinic—and me. He comes to visit every so often. And snag some kibble."

"He just roams the town?"

"No, he really doesn't. He comes and goes, but always seems to have a destination in mind. Good-hearted people have tried to take him, but no one's been able to keep him from wandering off." She snapped her fingers. "Come here, boy."

The dog's hackles lowered, and his ears perked up.

He padded over and let Katherine scratch his head, but he never took his gaze from Dominic.

"He's looking at me like I'd be a tasty morsel," Dominic said.

She chuckled. "He knows where his food is. Buddy, this is Dominic." She glanced up at him. "Hold your hand out so he can sniff it."

"You sure he won't just take it off?"

"I'm sure."

Dominic obeyed and Buddy's ears once more lowered, but he crept forward and gave the hand a sniff, looked back at Katherine, then nosed Dominic's fingers.

"He wants you to scratch his head," she said.

Dominic complied and the dog gave his hand a sudden slurpy swipe. Dominic laughed. "All right, then. I guess we're friends now. Good boy."

"This way," Katherine said. Dominic followed Katherine and Buddy into the medical clinic. He refused to acknowledge feeling a little light-headed from the drugs still running through his system, but was infinitely glad he'd managed to keep his balance thus far.

She nodded. "My place is just up those stairs."

He winced. Stairs. Great. He hoped there was a handrail. There was and he managed to get up the steps without embarrassing himself. Barely.

The door opened into a small foyer with a kitchen to the right and a large den to the left. A hallway off the living area probably led to her bedroom. "There's another set of stairs that leads down to the clinic. I use that when I'm going to work. Most of the time I use the ones we just came up."

"Good to know."

Buddy went to the corner of the kitchen and sat while

Katherine filled the bowl with food and gave him fresh water. "Are you sure he's not yours?" Dominic asked.

"I'm sure." She shrugged. "I don't really have time for a dog." She paused. "I did make sure he's had all of his shots and I gave him a bath before I let him in my place, but he's a vagabond now."

"What about animal control?"

She shook her head. "What animal control? This is Timber Creek. I know that sounds weird after what I told you about our medical facilities and stuff, but it's still a very small town. Besides, like I said, Buddy seems to keep to a certain area. He's either out in the woods on the outskirts of town, or here."

"I think you've got yourself a dog."

She huffed. "Nope." But she gazed at the animal with a fond look in her eye. A look that turned troubled for a brief moment. Then she turned that look to him. "You've got to be hungry, too."

"I'm not too fond of kibble, so I think I'll pass."

She gave a light chuckle. "I'm not the best cook, but I can do better than kibble for you. I keep a lot of fresh fruit, veggies and lettuce for salads." She raised a brow. "But you kind of strike me as a steak and potatoes kind of man."

He laughed. "I enjoy a good salad as much as the next person, but I can order something and have it delivered. I don't want you to go to any trouble."

A smile curved her lips. "Order something and have it delivered? That's a lovely concept."

"Let me guess—you don't have that service here."

"I think the pizza place delivers. They have other stuff, too, like wings. The town spends most of its money on essential things."

"Like medical care and law enforcement?"

"Yes."

"Interesting. Okay, then I think I'll just take you up on that salad after all."

"Have a seat on the couch," she said, "and I'll get it fixed for you. Anything you don't like?"

He settled himself onto the couch and let out a quiet sigh and smothered the groan that wanted to escape. "Tomatoes and cucumbers. Can't stand either of them." Her laugh sent a strange warmth coursing straight to his heart.

"I think I can manage to leave those off," she said.

"Thank you."

"How about carrots, onions, olives, bacon, hard-boiled eggs and sliced ham? Ranch dressing? Oh, and I do have some sharp cheese."

"All good." He leaned his head back and closed his eyes. "Can I help you?" *Please say no.*

"Ah…it doesn't look like you're up for that. I'll manage."

The amusement in her tone had him peeling one eye open. She shook her head, turned and headed for the refrigerator. "This place isn't very big," she said. "It's just a one bedroom, one bath, but there's enough room for you on the couch. It's a comfortable one and sleeps well when you add a pillow and a blanket."

"I'll be fine." And there was that word again. How many times had he used the word *fine* in the last three hours?

"Okay, just know that I'll be checking on you during the night, so don't get all jumpy if you see me leaning over you with a flashlight shining in your eyes."

Well, that sounded like a prescription for "how to make a headache worse." "Not a problem," he mumbled.

He closed his eye and listened to her working in the kitchen while his heart hummed a message that said it could get used to this whole domestic scene.

He did his best to shut that down. He wasn't here for fun and games and definitely not for romance. He had a killer to track down and he needed to do it fast.

Because while his head throbbed and he desperately needed rest to heal, his heart beat with the pain of a deep wound of grief that wouldn't begin to mend until Carl's killer was behind bars.

THREE

Katherine carried the salad into the den, spotted her patient asleep on the couch and did an about-face back to the kitchen where she returned the food to the refrigerator. She turned to Buddy who sat in the doorway. "I guess we should let him sleep while he can, huh?" She whispered the words to the dog and he tilted his head as though listening. "Yeah, I think so, too."

She snagged her laptop from the desk in the corner of the den and carried it into the kitchen. Buddy settled himself on the floor and placed his nose on her left foot. While he and her guest snoozed, Katherine caught up on her paperwork from the day before.

Briefly, she debated postponing her three-day minivacation if she was going to be working the whole time, but decided to see how things played out over the next day or so.

Next, she turned her attention to her phone and pulled up her father's number. Would he have his phone on? Would it be charged? Did he still have it or had someone managed to steal it?

She never knew from day to day if she'd be able to get in touch with him. He was one of Asheville's homeless. And not because she hadn't tried to get him to move into the home he had here in town—or even with her. But he'd refused. And that broke her heart, but it wasn't like she could force the man to do something he didn't want to do. Sometimes he found a shelter to sleep in and managed to charge the phone she'd gotten him and finally convinced him to keep on his person.

Katherine dialed the number and it went to voice mail on the first ring. So, the phone was either dead or off. "Hi, Dad, it's me. I'm just calling to see if I can bring you some food or anything. Give me a call or shoot me a text to let me know how you are."

She hung up, said a prayer for her father and her most recent patient, then turned to the laptop.

After a couple of hours, Buddy walked to the door and sat. Katherine opened it and let him out the back exit where he could go down the steps and into the small fenced-in grassy area she'd had put in when she'd taken the apartment.

She hadn't intended it to be used for a dog but figured he might as well have access to it if he needed it. Two months ago, she'd also put in the doggie door in the gate and Buddy figured it out so fast, she'd wondered if Mr. White had had one for him.

She bit her lip and frowned. Dominic's teasing about the fact that he thought she had a dog worried her. Should she take Buddy in and keep him? Be his permanent home? He seemed to like her—or at least the brand of dog food she provided, but, like she'd told Dominic, other people had tried and Buddy seemed to like being on his own with the occasional stop for food and water at her place.

And besides, she didn't need the full-time responsibility of a dog. Right?

Right.

Maybe.

Ugh. *Quit thinking about it and focus.*

She scrolled to the next patient and stopped. Grace Upworth. She was pregnant with a little boy and due any day now. Katherine sent an email to the doctor on duty to let him know to check on the woman tomorrow morning and he responded almost immediately that he'd been called out of town on a family matter. I know it's your day off, he said, but if you could check on her, that would be great.

Katherine shook her head. She had a feeling she was going to be working more than vacationing over the next three days. Sure, I'll take care of it. She hit Send then rose and walked into the den to find Dominic still sleeping soundly. He only gave her an annoyed grunt when she checked his eyes. His pupils were still even. That was a good sign. Maybe he was going to escape any serious residual effects of being knocked in the head. She left him alone and went back to her laptop.

A short time later, her phone pinged, and she glanced at the text. Do you have some more of that sample cream for the poison ivy? I'm still looking for a job and just can't afford it. I'm sorry.

Stacy Mann. A single mother with an eight-year-old who'd tangled with the wrong kind of vines. I believe I have a couple of the smaller tubes. Let me run down and check and I'll let you know. If I have some, I'll send you the code and you can pick them up at your convenience. She and the other doctors used the box on the side of the building for after-hours patient pick-ups. The code was changeable with each use and completely private.

Thank you, Katherine. Don't know what we'd do without you.

Katherine smiled and thought about what her former boss at the hospital in Asheville would say if he knew she gave out her personal number to a select few of her patients. She could almost hear the shouts that used to cause her ears to ring and was so glad to be out of *that* environment. Mostly.

But being a small-town doctor fit her needs at the moment and she was glad for the opportunity. The minutes ticked past into an hour. Then another.

She rose and checked on Dominic once more. When she lifted his eyelid and shone the light to gauge his pupil reaction, he frowned at her, blinked, then let her finish her miniexam. "Sorry for the light," she said. "I think you're okay, though."

He ran a hand over his face. "How long was I out this time?"

"A few hours. You missed that fabulous salad I made."

His belly rumbled loud enough to send pink into his cheeks. "I think my stomach is expressing it's unhappiness about that very thing."

"Not to worry. It's in the refrigerator. I'll get it for you, then I have to run downstairs real quick to grab some samples for a patient of mine."

"I'll come in the kitchen. Is the beast still here?"

"Beast?" A quiet laugh escaped her. "No, he's gone."

"Okay. Thanks."

"Sure." He rose and she was glad to see he didn't stumble or sway on his way into the kitchen. "How's the head?"

"Better, I think. It's annoying, but not pounding quite as hard."

"That's good news. I'll be right back, okay?"

"Of course." He cleared his throat. "Thank you, Katherine. This is above and beyond and I really do appreciate it."

She smiled. "I'm happy to do it. I won't be long." She zipped down the steps, her heart pounding. That look in his eyes…

When was the last time someone had looked at her like that?

Never? But that was her own fault. It wasn't like she gave men the opportunity. She hated the fact that she found it difficult to trust the opposite sex, but she couldn't seem to help it. She knew not all men were like her father.

But old habits and years of distrust died hard.

And yet, there was something about Dominic…

He's a patient. That's all.

Her mind got it, even accepted it, but her heart was on a different page in the book. In spite of the fact that she gave her number out to certain patients, she'd never invited one into her home like this before. What made Dominic so special? True, he was handsome in a rough kind of way with his five-o'clock shadow, blue eyes and wavy dark hair, but she'd been around good-looking guys before.

None of whom she'd brought home to keep an eye on while they healed. Maybe it was the fact that they'd dodged bullets together. Or that he was mourning the loss of his partner and his sorrow had tugged on her heartstrings so hard, she'd lost all sense. Whatever it was, it was freaking her out just a bit. Getting out of the apartment allowed her to take a step back and draw in a deep breath.

Focus.

She walked into the clinic and flipped on the light. She opened the safe and grabbed the keys. The medications were locked in the back and the keys were kept in the safe when no one was in the building.

A noise at the door paused her. She shut the safe and walked to the patient entrance. The clinic wasn't open on the weekends. If there was an emergency, everyone knew they had to go to the hospital or ring the doctor on call.

Katherine glanced at the alarm keypad and noted it was off. She'd turned it off when she'd escorted Dominic into the building and had forgotten to reset it. Well, that wasn't good, but not tragic. Even if anyone managed to get inside, they couldn't get to any narcotics. But the computers and other equipment would bring a pretty penny. Weaving the keys between her fingers to use as a weapon, she crept over to the door and looked out.

No one was there and she drew in a steadying breath. "Paranoid much?" she muttered.

But the sound from the back door sent her nerves humming. She reached for her cell phone only to remember she'd left it upstairs, planning to just grab the meds and lock them in the box located outside the clinic, then head back to text Stacy the medication was there.

Katherine approached the door cautiously, but thought she'd locked it. She got close enough to see the dead bolt was thrown and relaxed a fraction.

Until she saw the outline of the person at the door.

The knob jiggled and the shadow disappeared for

a moment before returning. A gloved fist smashed through the glass pane and reached for the dead bolt.

Heart hammering, pulse racing, Katherine picked up the nearest chair and slammed it on the arm. His scream echoed through the area, but he snagged the bottom rung and shoved the chair back at her. The top edge caught her hard in the stomach and she went down with a grunt. Katherine scrambled to her feet and raced to the phone on the receptionist's desk just as he flipped the dead bolt and stepped inside.

Dominic jerked at the thud that had come from below him. He'd finished the salad, washed his plate and returned to the couch to think about his witness turned fugitive and how to find him. Noah Bennett was twenty years old and, as far as Dominic was concerned, not the brightest bulb in the chandelier.

But he wasn't stupid, either.

Now Dominic waited, listening, wondering if he should go check on Katherine. Another crash from downstairs sent him to his feet too fast and he had to pause a second for the room to stop spinning. Then he bolted for the kitchen and the stairs that would take him down to the clinic.

He pushed through the door at the bottom to see Katherine wrestling with a dark-clad figure who wore a ski mask.

"Hey!" Dominic's shout distracted the intruder just enough to allow Katherine to get in a good punch to the person's face. Her attacker's head snapped back, he let out a cry, then spun to shove past Dominic and dart out the open door.

Dominic didn't bother to try to stop the guy. He

wouldn't last three seconds in hand-to-hand combat at the moment. Besides, he was more worried about the doctor. He rushed to her and snagged her arm. "Are you okay?"

"Yes." She sucked in a deep breath and swept her hair from her face. "I think so." Sirens sounded and she hurried to the door. "That'll be the sheriff, Creed Payne."

Dominic followed her to look out the broken window. "When did you call the cops?"

"After he knocked me down with the chair, it took him a couple of seconds to get in. By then I'd run to the phone and dialed 911. He caught me pretty quick, but I yelled at Susan to send help ASAP."

"Susan?"

"The dispatcher."

"*The* dispatcher? As in one?"

"One of four. Three of them work eight hour shifts and then there's a weekend dispatcher."

Dominic pressed a hand to his aching head. Small-town life. He'd never survive. He could only hope that the sheriff was at least competent. Katherine opened the door and the same tall man who'd come looking for them on the ranch stepped inside still wearing his black Stetson. He was followed by two deputies. Dominic remembered Ben Land from that morning, as well. The other deputy was a woman with dark curly hair and midnight-colored eyes. She was pretty with a sturdy build.

"This is Regina Jacobson," Katherine said.

"Good to meet you."

Regina nodded.

"You okay, Katherine?" the sheriff asked.

"Yes, but the guy who broke in took off. Someone might want to see if they can find him."

Regina looked at Ben. "You take the east end. I'll head west." To him and Katherine, she asked, "Any idea what he looks like?"

"Dark clothes, ski mask and black gloves," Katherine said. "And he smelled like onions. He might have eaten at the diner before he came here."

"Would be a good place to keep an eye on the clinic while he was planning whatever it was he was planning."

"Exactly."

"I'm headed east," Ben said. "We'll be in touch."

They left without the sheriff having to say a word. Dominic found that impressive. The sheriff eyed him. "They're good at what they do."

He had a feeling the sheriff was, too. That was a huge relief. "Glad to hear it."

"Walk me through what happened," the man said to Katherine. He took off his Stetson and raked a hand over his sandy-blond hair.

"I came down to get some medicine for a patient to put in the box outside." She told the story in about five minutes. Dominic listened, mentally filing each detail.

"That it?" Creed asked when she stopped speaking.

"That's it. He ran off when Dominic came down."

"Glad you were here," the man said.

"Me, too, Sheriff."

"Call me Creed." To Katherine, he asked, "What do you think he was after? Drugs?"

She shrugged. "I guess. I don't know what else he might be…after." She finished that last word with her gaze on Dominic. His jaw tightened. "You think he was trying to get to me." The words came out flat. "To finish the job."

Creed nodded. "Makes sense." He tapped his lips with the pen then turned back to Katherine. "Or he was a junkie, saw you in here and thought he could convince you to hand over something for a quick fix."

Katherine frowned. "Maybe, but I don't think so. He was too controlled. And well prepared. I didn't get the feeling that he was a junkie, however, I have nothing but my gut to base that on."

"Your gut's good enough for me," Creed said. "All right. I've got some plywood at the office. I'll bring some over and board up that window on the door. Think you ought to consider upgrading to a steel door."

"Hey, I've been asking to do that since I moved here. Talk to the city council members."

"I might just do that," the man muttered. He looked at Dominic. "How long you going to be around?"

"Until I catch up with the man I'm chasing. Two other marshals should be in town by now to help out."

Dominic nodded. "They stopped by and introduced themselves. Also, I saw the short news clip. You got a name for us yet?"

"Noah Bennett."

"Noah Bennett!" Katherine's startled yell bounced off the ceiling.

Both she and the sheriff looked nonplussed. Dominic blinked. "Yeah, why? You know him?"

Katherine swallowed and rubbed her palms against her thighs. "You could say that I know him. He's my brother."

FOUR

Katherine stood frozen trying to process what the marshal was saying. "What's Noah done?" Her mother hadn't bothered to let her know anything was wrong. Not that she was surprised by that, but obviously something was very, very wrong and her twenty-year-old brother was somehow involved.

Dominic's eyes had turned frosty at her revelation. "Killed my partner for one."

She gaped. "No, he didn't. He wouldn't."

Creed's gaze bounced from her back to Dominic. Then back to her. "You haven't seen or talked to Noah in a very long time, Katherine."

Like she needed the reminder. "It's been three years, but not because I haven't tried."

Creed nodded. "A lot can happen in three years. A person can change. Noah's not the awkward teenager anymore."

"No, but you don't go from taking in strays and nursing them back to health to shooting federal officers."

"You'd be surprised at what people do," Dominic muttered.

"Not Noah." She crossed her arms and met him glare for glare.

Creed's radio squawked and he pressed the button. "Go ahead."

"We've lost the suspect." Regina's voice filled the room. "We questioned several people who were on the street and one person said he saw the man come out from behind the clinic, hop into a truck and take off. I've already requested security footage from the deli and the hotel across the street."

"Good work. Anything else?"

"I spoke to Allison at the diner. She said she remembers a guy sitting near the window who seemed more interested in scrolling on his phone than eating. I asked her to describe him and she said he kept his ball cap on and didn't look at her much when she took his order. She said she'd never seen him in town before and that he had pretty hands."

"Pretty hands?" Creed frowned.

"You know, like manicured. Like he didn't do much manual labor—or if he did, he took care of his hands."

"Right. Get the word out we're looking for Noah Bennett."

Katherine groaned and pressed her palms to her eyes. "Creed, please…"

"Sorry, Katherine. You know I have to do this."

That was the problem. She *did* know. And had the roles been reversed, she would have done exactly the same thing. She gave him a sharp nod, then met Dominic's gaze. "Okay, then find him and he can tell you exactly why he ran from you. Because he must have had a good reason."

Something flickered in his eyes, but he covered it

quickly and shook his head. "All I know is one night, we had him in protective custody at a safe house in Asheville. The next morning, he was gone."

"Protective custody for what?"

"He witnessed a murder and in order to save his own hide from a trip to prison, he agreed to turn state's evidence."

Katherine really needed to sit down. "Okay, I need to find some of those samples and put them in the box for my patient. Then, can we go back upstairs to discuss this?"

"Of course."

Moving on autopilot, Katherine did what she needed, then headed for her apartment. Dominic moved more slowly, but he followed, with Creed bringing up the rear.

Once they were all upstairs, she detoured into the kitchen and snagged her phone to text Stacy that the samples were in the box. She took a seat on the couch next to Dominic and Creed took the recliner. "I'll just call Noah and get him to come here so we can figure this all out."

"He doesn't have a phone," Dominic said. "It was taken from him when he agreed to the terms of the protection."

Katherine drew in a slow breath and set her phone on the end table. "All right. Then please, finish filling me in."

Dominic closed his eyes for a moment as though getting his thoughts together. "Okay, I'm going to tell you what I know. If I get something wrong, correct me."

"Sure."

"Noah left home shortly after his eighteenth birthday. He said he had to get away from his parents."

Katherine swallowed and shook her head. She honestly couldn't blame her brother for that.

"He wound up sleeping in his car and driving for a food delivery service until he saved enough to rent a room. He moved in with a guy who was associated with some very nasty people."

"Let me guess," Katherine said, "he pulled Noah into whatever it is he's in trouble for now."

"I'm not sure how much pulling he had to do, but yeah. Noah got involved."

"So, how did he wind up with you?" Creed asked.

"He witnessed his boss shooting someone. It scared him bad enough that he went to the cops."

"Oh." Katherine rubbed her eyes trying to process everything.

Creed leaned forward and clasped his hands between his knees. "What was he doing that was illegal?"

"He was involved with a stolen-car ring. He and some of the others would steal cars, then drive them back to the warehouse where they were broken down to sell for parts. According to an officer who was undercover, on the other side of the warehouse, there was a drug ring going on. Noah denied knowing anything about the drugs. He said he only dealt with the cars. And maybe that's true, I don't know. But the officer had enough on Noah to send him away for quite a while and used that to convince Noah to turn state's evidence."

"So," Katherine said, "he went to the cops and they used that to blackmail him into testifying."

"Pretty much."

"Wow."

"I know. It sounds like a betrayal, but when you're desperate to bring down murderers, sometimes you do things that seem…wrong. Nothing against the law, of course, but—"

"But," Creed said, "betraying a kid's trust and putting him between a rock and a hard place are acceptable things to do in order to catch a killer."

Dominic sighed. "Yeah."

Creed looked at Katherine. "You know you'd do the same thing if it was you chasing a murderer. You worked with law enforcement long enough to know how it works."

"I know. I get it," she said. "I don't like it, but I get it. Go on."

"When Noah saw the evidence against him," Dominic said, "he was furious at first. He started denying everything and tried to backpedal, talk his way out of the situation. But when he finally realized the evidence and the charges weren't going away and his public defender wasn't worth much, he agreed to turn state's evidence and testify to everything he'd seen—and name names. After hearing his story, several arrests were made related to an organized crime ring and Noah became *the* most important witness in the case. Right now, a very powerful crime boss is sitting in prison and he's not happy about it."

"Hence the hit on Noah and your protecting of a federal witness," Creed said.

"Yes."

Katherine frowned. "Then why did he run?"

"We're not exactly sure, but…" Dominic ran a hand over his jaw and sighed. "There were a couple of… incidents."

"What kind?"

"Someone breached the safe house location and tried

to grab him. We have no idea how the person found out where we were keeping Noah, but it scared him." He paused. "To be honest, it scared us all. But we got him out of there and to another place. We took even more precautions and Noah seemed to relax a bit." He shook his head. "But something spooked him, I guess, and he took off."

"I can understand him being scared and running, but he wouldn't shoot anyone." She frowned. "It simply doesn't make sense. He was cooperating in order to avoid prison. Why would he shoot the people trying to help him do that?"

Dominic shrugged. "I can think of quite a few reasons. He was tired of being cooped up and thought he'd get his freedom when he had the chance. He got scared and figured he'd be better off on his own and had to get rid of two of the marshals trying to stop him. I don't know." He narrowed his eyes at her. "But I do know that my partner is dead, and your brother is to blame for it."

Katherine flinched and even Creed shot him a narrow-eyed look. Dominic immediately regretted his harsh words, but the sight of Carl on the ground, dead, was front and center in his mind.

"Tell me about Carl," Katherine said. "What was he like?"

Dominic's pulse settled a fraction at her calm words. "He was kind of a shy guy, but he loved practical jokes. He was smart and funny with a dry sense of humor— and he was one of my best friends."

"Wife?" Katherine asked. "Kids?"

"No, he hung out with me and two of my buddies, Leon Yates and Evan Kennedy, when we weren't working—and sometimes another marshal buddy of ours, Owen Charles. You met him at the hospital with Beth."

"Right."

"But it was mostly just the four us. We are—were—tight. Best friends." He turned his phone so she could see the wallpaper picture of the four of them. "This is us."

"Good-looking group of guys, there," she said, her voice soft.

"Thanks." Emotion tightened his throat and he cleared it. "Sorry. I don't know how I'm going to tell the guys that Carl's dead. I should have already called them. I'll need to do that shortly."

"I'm so sorry," Katherine said, "more sorry than I can even put into words, but I just can't believe Noah's responsible for that."

Dominic's heart chilled. "I understand that he's your brother, but sometimes our family members do things we don't understand—or like."

"Yes, I figured that out when my mother cheated on my father, then left him—and me—to marry the guy without one glance back. It was also driven home that family members often make stupid choices. Like when they insist they'd rather live on the streets as a homeless person than get help and have a life with someone who loves them. So, yes, I understand family can disappoint and do things that we don't understand or like, but I just don't see Noah doing this."

"Katherine—" Creed's voice was soft, but Katherine didn't look at him. She held Dominic's eyes and he knew he didn't manage to hide his own flinch. Whoa. He never would have thought—

"I'm sorry," he said. "I didn't know."

"How could you?" She waved a hand. "I didn't tell you that for sympathy, but to express that I don't have blinders on when it comes to my family. If I thought Noah was responsible for the death of your partner, I'd be the first one in line to track him down."

Dominic sighed, his head pounding a harder rhythm, sending faint waves of nausea through him. He did his best to ignore the pain and focus. Katherine had stated facts about her family that he couldn't imagine. His own parents had been married for over thirty years before his father had been wounded in the line of duty.

His phone buzzed, interrupting him. He glanced at the screen. "Carl's parents are thirty minutes away from the hospital. I need to get over there and be there for them." He paused. "I guess I'll call Leon and Evan after I speak with them."

"I'll go with you," Katherine said.

He hesitated. "If I'm a target then I probably need to find another place to stay—and you need to keep your distance."

"I don't think that's necessary. At least not tonight. They failed on this attempt so will have to pull back, regroup and figure out if they're going to try again."

"They'll try again," Creed said. "I've put my deputies on high alert. We'll keep this place under surveillance for as long as you're here." He looked at Katherine. "Better dust off your piece."

"Consider it dusted."

Creed stood. "Come on. I'll give you a ride to the hospital. Hopefully, that'll keep anyone after you at bay for the moment."

Dominic rubbed his eyes in lieu of nodding. "Fine. Thank you."

Katherine's brown eyes narrowed on him and he had a feeling she knew how rotten he was feeling. The fact that she didn't suggest he forget going to the hospital said how well she was at reading people. Reading him.

It unnerved him slightly, but then he shifted all of his attention on getting out the door and down the steps without falling on his face.

FIVE

Katherine stood at the entrance to the morgue with Creed while Dominic greeted his partner's parents. The grief on their faces broke her heart—and stirred a smidgeon of jealousy. She'd thought she was past that emotion, that she'd accepted the environment she'd been born into—and risen above. Apparently, she had more work to do because, not for the first time in her life, she wondered what it would be like to be loved unconditionally by the two people who'd brought her into the world?

Unfortunately, she'd never know for sure, but thankfully, Creed's family had given her a taste of it as a teen when they'd let her live with them during the worst of her father's binges. Creed had become her older, protective brother and she loved him for it.

"Kat? You okay?"

He'd caught her watching. Had he noticed her longing? "Sure, I'm fine."

The knowing look in his eyes said he wasn't fooled. "You mentioned your dad earlier. How is he?"

She raised her chin at him. "Still living on the streets in Asheville, begging change off the tourists to feed his alcoholism."

He grimaced. "I'm sorry."

"Me, too." She paused. "The last time I saw him, I offered to pay for him to go to rehab, get himself cleaned up. I think I've convinced myself if I could just get him away from the alcohol and back to working with his hands, he'd remember how happy it made him."

"He's got a lot of talent when it comes to woodworking. Is he not interested in doing it anymore?"

"That's the sad thing. I think he is. I see the longing in his eyes when I bring it up, but he—" She sighed and shook her head. "I think he's depressed. I think he's consumed with grief over losing my mother and guilt over everything that landed him where he is. I think he feels like he doesn't deserve to be happy or— loved." The last word caught in her throat and nearly choked her. How she wanted to love and help the man she called Dad.

"I know, Kat. I know."

Dominic walked over to them and ran a hand down his pale face. "I think that was one of the most difficult things I've ever had to do in my life."

Katherine shoved aside the grief that always accompanied talking about her parents—especially her father—and laid a hand on his arm. "I can't imagine how hard it was to hear, but I know they were thankful you were here to tell them everything. To explain exactly what happened and how. At least they don't have any unanswered questions—other than who actually pulled the trigger."

He blinked. "That's exactly what his mother said— that she was glad there were no unanswered questions." He cleared his throat and she was glad he didn't refute her claim that they didn't know the shooter. "As a physician, I know you've had to deliver tragic news before."

"I have. And it never gets easier."

"Yeah." His husky voice touched her, and she wished she could do something to comfort him, but knew from experience there was nothing to say. This was a loss that would be with him forever. Time would help turn the shattering pain to a manageable ache, but for now, he would have to take one day at a time.

He drew in a deep breath. "All right, I need to think about our next move." He cut his gaze to Katherine. "Any ideas where Noah would run to if he was planning to hide out for a while?"

"No." At his frown, she sighed. "And yes, I would tell you if I knew, but, Creed's right. I haven't seen Noah in almost three years. He grew up in Asheville, so I recommend calling my mother and asking her."

"You don't want to do it?"

"Not if you want actual communication. She's more likely to talk to you than me."

"That sounds like some bad blood between you two."

"You could say that."

He raised a brow, but she didn't bother to elaborate. He already knew her mother had abandoned her family for another man. No sense in airing all of the dirty laundry at once. She gave him the number. "If she won't tell you, Noah's father might. His name is Pete Bennett. He's nice enough, just never around when Noah was little—or anytime really. He's a paramedic and works a lot of hours. He also prefers hanging out with the people he works with more than his family." She frowned. "I don't know why I just thought of this, but why would Noah be heading here? His home is in Asheville."

"Which is where we were protecting him," Dominic said. "Or rather on the outskirts. But it was a safe place." He raised a hand to head off any comment she might have about why Noah might have run in the first place. "This one was—I promise."

"So, why leave it?"

"No idea. He has no friends at all here?" Dominic asked.

"None that I've ever heard of him keeping in touch with." She rubbed her forehead. "I was thirteen when Noah was born. When I was fifteen, my mom started dropping him off to me every other weekend so that she and Pete could be alone." She shrugged. "They paid me a pittance, but I took it and got to know my little brother." She fought the emotion the memories brought to the surface. "Pete and my mother are very selfish people—I keep praying they'll change, but so far it hasn't happened. They're not necessarily intentionally cruel or mean—at least not to Noah—they're just entitled and think the world should revolve around them. I didn't want Noah to grow up that way. As soon as I could drive, I would get him as often as my mother would allow. We had some playdates with families, but, like I said, no one that I've ever heard him keeping in touch with."

Dominic nodded. "Give me your mom's number, and I'll see what I can find out."

She looked it up on her phone and shared the contact with him. Katherine studied the number she hadn't used in a very long time. "When he was sixteen, he was caught shoplifting," she said, her voice soft. "The officer was friends with my stepfather, and Noah got a slap on the wrist and some community service. About a week later, Noah called and asked if he could come live with me. I told him I'd talk to our mother about it." Katherine glanced up at the men and noted their intense attention. "She said no. She said, in fact, it would probably be better if I didn't contact Noah at all and let there be natural consequences to his actions." She gave a light scoff, remembering her anger, her sheer disbelief that her mother would refuse to let her help—or let her even *talk* to her brother. "I wanted to give him what I knew he wasn't getting from our mother. Guidance, love… *attention*. I even tried to call him, and Mom found out. I guess she had his phone or saw my number on the bill or maybe she scrolled through his phone when he wasn't looking. Anyway, she threatened to press charges if I tried to contact him in any way." She shrugged. "I was heartbroken, but if I didn't agree, I—" Katherine sighed and closed her eyes.

"You could have been arrested and lost your license," Dominic said.

"Yes." Tears gathered, but she refused to let them fall. "I wanted to be there for him, of course, but—" What was she doing sharing such personal information with a complete stranger? She must be more tired than she thought. "But it didn't work out that way." She drew in a deep breath. "Anyway, I agree we need to find him. I'm just afraid it isn't going to be easy." She paused. "If he was heading this way on purpose—and it looks like he was—then maybe he was coming to me for help." She finally looked up to find Dominic and Creed watching her.

Dominic's jaw tightened. "Or maybe he's the one who tried to break into the clinic tonight because he needs money."

"I don't believe that." Not Noah. The sweet little boy who used to crave her attention. Who'd climb into her lap and beg her to tell him stories about dinosaurs and dump trucks.

"I understand that," Dominic said, "but, in spite of your realistic viewpoint when it comes to your family, I still say you're not exactly objective."

She bit back a protest. As much as she didn't want to admit it, he might be right. "I guess we just need to find him and ask him."

Dominic's eyes narrowed and Katherine turned to see Carl's parents standing just outside the viewing area. Carl's mother fell into her husband's arms, and Katherine wanted to weep with them. "Yeah," Dominic said, "we sure do need to ask him, preferably before he kills any more of my friends—or me."

Katherine went white and Creed stiffened, his gaze sharp. Regret hit Dominic before the last word left his lips. What was wrong with him? He held up a hand. "I'm sorry. I'm sorry. That was uncalled for." He kept spouting words he needed to apologize for when normally, he'd never say anything to intentionally hurt another person. Then again, he'd never had a partner murdered, either. But that was no excuse not to control his tongue.

"It really was," Katherine said. "Please don't judge Noah guilty before he has a chance to explain why he ran."

Dominic sighed and rubbed his eyes. "I'll do my best." He stood. "I'll call your mom now."

"She'll be sleeping. She might not be very happy—or cooperative—if you wake her up."

"This can't wait."

"I know. Just warning you."

"If I have to, I'll go pay her a visit."

Katherine nodded and he dialed the number. When it went straight to voice mail, he didn't bother leaving a message. He texted Beth and Owen the information and suggested a home visit would be in order. Owen responded that he'd let the director know.

When Dominic looked up, he spotted Carl's parents leaving the viewing area. "Excuse me." He went to them and hugged them one more time. "I'm going to find the person who did this," he said, stepping back from Carl's mother. "I won't stop until I find him."

She nodded then leaned in to squeeze him tight one more time. "Thank you. Please be safe. You've been such a good friend to Carl—to our entire family—we couldn't bear to lose you, too."

Like he'd just promised Katherine, he said, "I'll do my best. Let me know when the funeral is, and I'll keep you updated on our progress finding the killer." He walked them out of the hospital and turned to find Katherine and Creed behind him. The lights behind them wavered and he blinked.

Katherine placed a hand on his arm. "Dominic? You okay?"

"I think my head's had about all it can take today."

"I'm impressed it's lasted this long."

"Come on," Creed said, "I'll take you two back to Katherine's so you can get some rest. Then I'll have my deputies start canvassing the town and see if we can find Noah."

Dominic's phone buzzed. He glanced at the screen and let out a groan. "I just need to take this."

"Sure," Katherine said.

Creed nodded. "We'll wait for you by the door."

"Thanks." He swiped the screen. "Hi, Leon." Leon Yates, his best friend since middle school.

"Is it true?" Leon asked. "Is Carl dead?"

A sharp blast of grief rendered Dominic speechless for a brief second before he cleared his throat. "Yes. It's true. He is." Emotion nearly cost him his composure, cutting off his words for a moment. When he could speak again, he said, "I'm sorry I didn't call you. I've just been trying to deal with everything and figure out who did this."

"It's okay, man, but, I'm just… I don't know what to say."

"I know. His parents are here now making arrangements and…stuff."

"What happened?" Leon asked, his voice hoarse.

"I'm not a hundred percent sure, but we're fairly certain it was a fugitive who managed to get his hands on a gun."

"I see. Maybe this is a dumb question, but can I do anything?"

Could he? "No, nothing right now. At least not that I can think of. Carl's parents are here and will have to stay a couple of days to get…everything settled." He needed to find them a hotel. Did Timber Creek even have one? He could let Leon take care of that, but it would probably be easier if he just asked Katherine for the information. And, if there was a local hotel, he probably needed to check in as well and let Katherine have her home back. The thought of everything that needed doing turned the dial up on his pounding head. "Look, I've got to go. I'll catch up with you later."

"Keep me in the loop, will you? Even if it's just a text."

"Sure." He paused. "Actually, wait. I thought of one thing you can do."

"Anything."

"Tell Evan for me if he doesn't already know." Had he ever been a bigger wimp in his life? Probably not. But Leon was there. He could tell Evan in person.

"Of course."

"Thanks. I'll talk to you later."

They said their goodbyes and hung up. When he turned back to Katherine and Creed, they were watching him. Katherine had a particularly deep frown on her face, but she simply asked, "Are you ready to call it a night?" She paused. "Or is it morning?"

Creed glanced at his watch. "There are a couple of more hours until morning. We can all get some sleep if we leave now."

"Works for me," Dominic said. He was quite sure if he didn't lie down soon, he'd simply fall over and that would be that. Before he embarrassed himself, he'd better start listening to his body.

Thankfully, Creed was parked right by the entrance of the hospital and Dominic was able to slide into the back seat with only a small groan.

"I've got some pain pills at home that should work for you," Katherine said, her voice low.

"Maybe a half."

"Hm."

When they pulled into the clinic parking lot, the two deputies who'd gone after the shooter were waiting in their cruisers. Regina and Ben. They stepped out and Dominic noted the respect on their faces as Creed approached them.

His door opened distracting him from the officers. Katherine stood there with her hand outstretched. "Come on. Hold on to me so you don't face-plant into the asphalt."

"You're not very good for my ego, you know that?"

She chuckled. "I think your ego might be able to survive a few hits."

"Hey, now…"

"I'm kidding." Her eyes captured his. "You strike me as a very humble man. A good man."

He swallowed. "Well…thanks."

"A misguided and wrong-about-my-brother man, but even good men make mistakes."

He laughed, then groaned. "Please, don't make me do that. It hurts." He took her hand and let her pull him out of the seat. He found his feet and paused a moment, willing his head to settle. At least that's what he told himself. The truth was, he didn't mind holding her hand. "The truth is, you make me want to be wrong about Noah."

She drew in a silent breath and held his gaze. "Thank you for that."

When he could walk a straight line, he followed her into the clinic with Creed and the deputies bringing up the rear.

Katherine directed him to the couch, and he dropped onto it with a soft grunt that escaped in spite of his efforts to hold it in.

"I'll just get that pain pill for you," Katherine said.

"Half. I can't be loopy."

"Right."

She disappeared into the back of the house while Regina and Ben settled on the love seat and Creed took the recliner. Katherine was back in a minute with half a pill and a bottle of water. "Any allergies?" she asked.

"Penicillin."

"Then we're good."

He nodded and downed the pill then looked at Katherine. "I think I need to go ahead and move to a hotel."

She frowned. "What? Why?"

"Because whoever is determined to finish the job made it very clear that he doesn't care who gets in the way. I don't want to be here and present a danger to you."

"I'm sure you would have mentioned it if you knew," she said, "so I'm assuming the other marshals haven't made any progress on finding the shooter."

"No. Nothing. It's like he's disappeared." He studied her. "Or there's someone here in town helping him."

SIX

Katherine stiffened and narrowed her eyes. "Are you saying I'm hiding him?" She stood, pointing a finger at him. "Don't you dare. Don't you even *dare*. I've been with you from the moment I found you and Carl—except when I was being attacked downstairs. I did not arrange for my brother to slip away into a hideout." Katherine shook, her tenuous hold on her temper slipping. "Really?"

"No. No, I don't think you're hiding him. At least not deliberately. But I wonder if you know something—and you just don't realize it."

"That's the dumbest thing I've ever heard." Katherine was nearly vibrating, her anger growing with each word that came out of his mouth.

He groaned. "I'm really trying not to put my foot in my mouth again and it's not working. I'm not expressing this right. Let me get my thoughts together so I can say what I mean without coming across like an ungrateful idiot."

"That might be a good idea."

Creed and the deputies sat in silence, all watching with matching frowns.

Dominic pressed a hand to his head then sighed. "I didn't mean you were deliberately hiding him from us, just that you might know of a place he would go, but just haven't thought of it yet. That's all."

Well, that was a tad better and she supposed it was a fair thought on his part. Her ire faded. Slightly. "I'll tell you what. You get some rest, and I'll think on it."

Dominic had the grace to simply nod. His eyelids drooped and she could tell the medicine was starting to kick in. She tilted her head at the other three to follow her into the kitchen. Once there, she looked at Creed. "What do you think? You've met Noah, even spent a good amount of time with him when he was younger. You think he could have done this?"

Creed held up a hand. "I can't make that call, Kat, you know that. I haven't seen the kid in three years, either."

"Right," she whispered. "Where would he go if he came back?"

"The only place I can think of is here. To see you." He hesitated. "What about the guys he used to hang out with during the summer?"

"I have no idea who they were. No. Wait! Patrick. Mark and Grace Upworth's nephew. He's still around town, isn't he? Didn't they used to hang out some?"

"Yeah, now that you mention his name, it's ringing some bells. I think so. I'll ask around. In the meantime, you keep an eye out." He shook his head. "I still say he was coming to see you."

And yet, she doubted it. "Maybe. You see what you can find out and I'll see if I can come up with some names. Maybe Patrick will know. Other than that, I'm clueless as to what to do."

"There were others, too, if I remember correctly.

They used to hang out in the parking lot of the diner during the summer."

"Yes," she said, the memories coming back slowly. "Do you know who the other kids were? I remember Patrick."

"Maybe." Creed patted her shoulder. "I'll see if I can track them down and find out if they've heard from Noah. In the meantime, you need to get some rest yourself. Ben and I'll patrol the town one last time. Regina can stay here and keep an eye on the place while you sleep. I'll call you in a few hours."

Katherine nodded. "Thank you, Creed."

"Of course. Lock up and call if you hear anything suspicious. There's nothing in the criminal handbook that says not to strike twice in the same night."

"Wow. Thanks. I'm sure I'll have no trouble falling asleep now."

"I've got you covered," Regina said. "Go. Rest."

Creed and Ben left, and Katherine rubbed her eyes. Then turned to Regina. "I've been meaning to ask you how your mother's doing."

The deputy shrugged. "She's got dementia. Some days are better than others. We hold on to those with everything we've got. Unfortunately, the bad days are becoming all too frequent. Lisa's with her most since she can work from home, but I give her breaks as often as I can."

Lisa, Regina's older sister. Katherine winced. "Ouch. And now you're having to put in even more hours babysitting me. Us."

Regina's lips curled in a tired smile. "It's all part of the job. A job I happen to love very much, so I don't mind."

"If there's anything I can do, please just ask."

"I will. Thanks."

Regina left and Katherine watched her position herself so she could see the entrance to the clinic as well as the side stairs leading up to the entrance of her home, Katherine checked on her patient-slash-houseguest. He'd stretched out, taking up the full length of her oversize couch. His cheek rested on one of the throw pillows. She grabbed a regular sleeping pillow and a clean case from the linen closet in the hall and returned to the den, debating whether or not she should disturb him.

She covered him with a blanket and discreetly checked the bandage on his head. Looked clean.

When she pulled back, his eyes were on her and she gave a small gasp. "Don't do that," she said.

"What?"

His mumble was strangely endearing.

"Sneak watch me."

"I wasn't sneaking, I promise. Just too tired to move."

A light chuckle escaped her. "I guess so." She sobered. "I promise, Dominic, I don't know where Noah would be around here, but I do have a few people that I can call. Just on the off chance that he would show up there. I seriously doubt it, but I'm guessing you want to cover all the bases?"

"I do."

"So, I'll do that first thing in the morning. Creed and I thought of a few guys Noah used to kind of hang around with, too. He's going to check with them."

"Good. Thank you."

She snagged the pillow. "Here, use this one. It's got to be more comfortable than that throw pillow."

"'Kay." He lifted his head and she exchanged the pillows. His lashes fluttered against his cheeks then rose once more. "I really didn't mean to make you mad when I questioned you about Noah. It's just part of the job sometimes."

"I know."

"Creed said he'd have someone watching the place, right?"

"Yes. Regina's outside, standing guard. When I'm ready to sleep, she'll come in. You can go back to sleep now."

"You, too, promise?"

"Yep."

"Good." And then he was out like she'd flipped a switch.

With a weary sigh, Katherine rose and headed for her shower. Once she was ready to grab a few hours of sleep, she texted Regina to come in then padded to the bedroom window and looked out. Her gaze scanned the areas behind the clinic.

Movement caught her attention and for a moment, she tensed. Then realized it was Buddy. He slipped in the doggy door and made his way up the stairs to her place. She returned to the kitchen and waited for him to come through the second doggy door. "Decided you needed some company tonight, huh?" He nudged her hand and she obliged his request with a few scratches behind his ears. "Okay, my friend, I need sleep. Are you staying or going?" He walked to the bed she'd set in the corner near his dishes and curled up on it. "All right, then. I'll see you in the morning."

She signaled Regina she was ready to sleep, and the woman made her way inside and took a seat at the kitchen table. "You have a dog whether you want to admit it or not."

"Hush your mouth."

A light chuckle escaped the deputy and Katherine rolled her eyes before they settled on the dog. She wasn't fooling anyone with her insistence that she didn't want a dog. With each passing day, Buddy was becoming more hers. Or she was becoming more his. Whatever the case, she was soon going to have to concede defeat and accept the fact that she had a dog. The truth was, she was glad he was there. Especially tonight.

Because if anyone tried to get in the clinic or her home, Buddy would most likely know before Regina.

Dominic woke to Katherine's hushed voice and the welcome smell of fresh coffee.

And a slightly pounding head. At least it was better than when he fell asleep.

Ignoring the pain and desperate for the coffee, he rolled to his feet and stood still a moment, making sure he wasn't going down. When nothing tilted, swayed or spun, he headed for the kitchen.

Katherine stood next to the coffee maker, phone pressed to her ear. "It's all right, Grace, you're going to be fine. I'll be there as fast as I can get there, I promise."

Buddy sat in his bed, watching her, but turned his attention to Dominic with a flick of his ears. Since the dog didn't move, Dominic figured he was safe to step inside. When Katherine turned, she smiled and gestured to the coffeepot, a mug, sugar, cream and a spoon on the counter.

And two ibuprofen tablets.

He forced himself to walk, instead of bolt, to the mug. But he filled it, snagged two sugar cubes from the container and stirred. Then sipped.

He could almost feel his brain kick into gear. With

a sigh, he popped the two pills, then turned to face this woman he couldn't seem to stop thinking about.

Only the fact that her brother might have been the one who'd killed Carl held him back. How could he be attracted to her? He had to keep his emotions on the back burner. Or at least make the effort to do so. The truth was, he was very drawn to Katherine and wished he'd met her under different circumstances.

His next course of action would be a shower.

Katherine hung up. "That was a patient of mine. She's nine months' pregnant and I want to go check on her."

"I thought you were off work."

She shot him a smile. "I did, too, but things change."

"Did I interrupt your vacation plans?"

"Just three days of reading good books, drinking coffee and eating too much chocolate."

"Sounds like a well-earned break. I'm sorry to interrupt it." A pause. "Your patients don't come to the clinic?"

"When they can drive, they usually do. But Grace lives on top of the mountain and doesn't drive in the snow."

He blinked. "Snow?" She pointed to the window and he noticed the fat flakes falling—and sticking—"Right. Snow." It had been snowing when he and Carl had run across the ranch in search of Noah—and found themselves targets. He cleared his throat. "So, you're okay driving up the mountain in that?"

She shrugged. "Won't be the first time. I have four-wheel drive and chains, so I'll be all right." She set her mug on the counter. "Regina left to get some rest and Ben is going to stay here with you to keep an eye on things. Dr. Trey George is in the clinic today and seeing patients. The broken pane has been replaced and a new door ordered. This one is a glass door, but one that won't break easy."

He blinked. "How long have you been up?"

She smirked. "Just an hour, but I'm efficient."

"No kidding."

"Well, it helps to know people. A good friend's husband owns the glass shop in town and he came by about thirty minutes ago and fixed it right up."

And he hadn't heard a thing. That was kind of scary. Then again, it *had* been downstairs. "I guess there really are advantages to living in a small town. And you make house calls, too."

"A few. In certain situations like Grace's." She set her mug in the sink. "So, I'm going to head up the mountain. Do you have everything you need?"

He frowned. "Yes, I think so. I have a change of clothing and toiletries in the go bag, so I should be good to go. Thank you."

"Then what's the frown for?" she asked.

"I guess I just feel a little out of the loop."

She studied him for a brief moment before gathering her keys, purse and medical bag. "I can see it's making you crazy to be benched at the moment, but you really do need to heal. I know it goes against everything in you, but the more you follow my instructions, the faster that'll happen with fewer lingering issues."

"I know." He really did. Didn't mean he had to like it, though.

She shot him one last smile and then she was gone. The scent that he'd come to associate with her lingered. A cross between vanilla and lavender. He couldn't put a name to whether it was her soap, shampoo or lotion, but he drew in a deep breath then headed for the bathroom.

Twenty minutes later, feeling almost back to normal now that he'd showered and put on a fresh change of clothes, he walked back to the couch. In spite of his desire to be in the middle of the action, he'd never forgive himself if he pushed and then someone got hurt because he passed out or something. But while he might not be able to be in the field, he could still work from the comfort of the couch.

He texted Beth and Owen. Could I get an update?

The three little dots appeared on his screen and finally her text came through. Owen's with me so I'm answering for both of us. We're still searching. No sign of him. He'll show up eventually, and we'll be here to grab him. A pause as three more dots blinked at him. Did the doctor have any more ideas?

No, he texted. Unfortunately not. Please keep me updated. Thanks.

Of course. Feel better.

He sent her a thumbs-up emoji and tossed his phone on the cushion next to him. He opened the laptop, logged in and started searching for everything he could find on Noah Bennett. Social media was going to be his biggest help. Maybe.

Within ten minutes, his head had started to pound, and he had to close his eyes. Apparently, laptops and concussions—even *slight* ones—didn't play well together. A knock on the door sounded and he opened his eyes. With his weapon in his right hand, he rose and walked to peer out the side window. Creed stood on the steps. Dominic shoved his gun into the holster and opened the door. "Sheriff?"

"It's Creed."

"Everything okay?"

"I think I've found someone who might know something about Noah. I thought if you felt up to it—and promise not to tell Katherine I came and got you—you might want to ride with me and ask a few questions."

"You thought right."

"How's the head?"

"Feeling better by the minute."

Creed studied him. "You're lying."

"Only a little."

"All right. Let's go."

SEVEN

It had taken Katherine longer than she'd anticipated to climb the winding mountain road, but she'd finally made it. The Upworth family ran a tubing business, and it looked like most of the town had turned out to play. Thankfully. She knew the business was struggling.

Mark and Grace Upworth had been married for fourteen years and this was their third child. A child who apparently wasn't big on patience when it came to meeting the world.

Mark stepped out of the house when Katherine climbed out of the Subaru. "Hurry. I think she's ready to push," he said, then disappeared back inside.

Oh, then. Her checkup had just turned into a delivery. Katherine grabbed her bag and rushed after him. She found Grace in the master bedroom in the throes of a contraction. Katherine waited until it passed before clasping the panting woman's hand. "Hey, how are you?"

"Good. I'm great. Ready to do this."

"How far apart?"

"Two minutes."

"Okay, I'm going to examine you. You know how this works."

"Yeah." Grace grinned at her before falling back onto the pillow. "I'm ready to meet him."

"Then let's get busy." Katherine checked the woman and laughed. "It's a good thing you're ready to meet him because he's sure ready to meet you. Push on the next contraction."

"Dad!" Mark froze and spun. Their oldest boy, Christopher, was thirteen. He stopped in the doorway. "I need you on the slope. Some dude said he made reservations, but I can't find them. He said he paid, too, but I can't find that, either. He's saying I'm lying and that I either let his kids on the slopes or he's going to call the cops and get a lawyer." The words tumbled from the teen's lips and Mark flinched.

He looked at Grace and Katherine, indecision written on his features. Grace shrugged. "Go see what's going on."

"But—"

"Go!" Another contraction hit her, and Katherine waited while the woman pushed.

The baby's head crowned, and she patted Grace's leg. "You're doing great, my friend."

Grace groaned and Mark shook his head. "No way. I'm not leaving."

"It's fine, Mark," Grace said. Then laughed. "I can't…believe we're…having this conversation…while I'm trying to have a baby." She met his gaze. "We can't afford for anything to go wrong. Not this season. If something happens…well, you know what this will do to us financially. Go."

Mark raked a hand down his face then looked at his son. "Tell him I'll be right there."

Christopher ran from the room. Katherine had

known they were struggling, but not to the extent it seemed they were. It made sense, though. It wasn't like Timber Creek was a big tourist area. Mark and Grace had to rely on local support and the occasional visitor for their business. She hoped the troublemaker wasn't a resident.

Grace's mother, a woman in her late fifties, stepped inside with Stephanie, Grace and Mark's youngest— soon to be middle—child. Stephanie was eight years old and her blue eyes were wide, taking it all in. "Mom, are you okay?"

"I'm fine, honey. Your baby brother will be here soon."

Stephanie scowled and crossed her arms. "I wanted a sister."

Grace let out a low laugh then closed her eyes.

"Go on, Mark," Grace's mother said. "I tried talking to him, even told him Grace was having a baby, but he clearly doesn't care. Grace is right. You don't need any negative publicity about this place. This is your make-it-or-break-it year. Go take care of the man."

Mark sighed and kissed his wife's forehead as another contraction hit her. He waited while she pushed.

"Dad!" Christopher called from the den. "He said he's calling the police and filing a report that we're stealing his money!"

"Put them on the slopes now. Let them go. Tell him your mother is having a baby and I'm not leaving her."

The teen's footsteps faded, and Mark turned back to Grace. "You can do this, honey. The faster the better, apparently."

Grace let out a chuckle that turned to a groan. Two minutes later, Katherine held a squirming, healthy boy in her gloved hands. She laid the baby in his mother's arms while Mark looked on in adoration.

Seconds later, footsteps pounded back into the house.

"Dad, he said he didn't care, he's already called the cops and they're on the way."

"Go on, Mark," Grace said, "you can get to know this little man a little later. Go help Christopher and get that guy taken care of."

Mark muttered something under his breath and stomped from the room. Katherine finished up with the new mother and then left everyone else alone while she cleaned up in the adjoining bathroom.

She couldn't help remembering the day Noah was born. She'd been thirteen years old and delirious with joy over the fact that she was going to finally have a sibling. Against her father's wishes, she'd ridden her bike to the nearest bus station six miles away and, armed with her minor-traveling-alone pass, had hopped on the bus she'd used upon occasion to visit her mother— when her father was too drunk to care or bother to stop her. She refused to admit that each time she visited, she wondered why she made the effort.

But this time was different. She'd arrived to the hospital in time to hold Noah when he was less than an hour old. The memory of kissing his little bald head and promising to love and protect him forever swooped in to taunt her now.

She'd done a pretty lousy job of keeping her promise. Tears blurred her vision.

"Katherine?" Grace's voice stiffened her spine and she sniffed back the tears.

"Coming." She dried her hands and returned to the room to find the baby sleeping and Grace looking radiant in spite of the worry lines creasing her forehead. "He's beautiful, Grace."

"I completely agree."

Katherine smiled then sat in the chair next to the bed. "Grace, you remember my brother, Noah, right?"

"Of course." Her face softened. "I saw the news. I'm so sorry."

"Thank you, but I don't believe Noah is the one who killed that marshal." She drew in a deep breath. "However, his actions, including running from protective custody, stealing a car and then disappearing, aren't helping his case. Does Mark's nephew Patrick still live around here? He and Noah were about the same age and I *think* they used to hang out when he stayed with me."

"Check with Mark, but the last I heard Patrick was working at Sam's Garage in town." She paused. "Or maybe it was the car wash. I don't remember. That kid seems to change jobs on a regular basis. He likes to play or keep his nose in his phone more than he likes to work."

Grace's mother walked back into the room with a sandwich and some chips. She set the plate on the end table and Grace yawned.

Katherine patted her hand and stroked a finger down the baby's downy-soft cheek. "What's his name?"

"Maxwell Alexander. We'll call him Max."

"A fine, strong name." Katherine rose. "I'm just going to run out to the slope and let Mark know everything is fine with you and Max and see if he can tell me how to find Patrick."

"Thank you for coming, Katherine. I never would have made it down the mountain. The thought of giving birth in the truck really didn't appeal." She shuddered.

"I'm sure. I'm glad it all worked out." She said her goodbyes and threw her bag in her vehicle before stuffing her phone into the pocket of her vest and heading down the small hill to the entrance to the tubing area.

During the time Katherine had arrived up until now, the parking lot had emptied out and there were only a few people left on the slope. Mark had hired several local high school students to help him run the place, but business wouldn't really pick up for another couple of weeks. Katherine was glad the baby had made his appearance one week earlier than expected.

The bottom of the run ended at the entrance of the lodge. Smoke billowed from the huge fireplace at the center of the building. Beyond the lodge was more wooded acreage that Mark and Grace planned to use to expand their business. Assuming they didn't lose it first.

At the top of the run, black inner tubes lined the fence. Christopher was busy helping one tuber onto his and gave him a slight shove, sending him whipping down the slope. When Christopher turned, he spotted Katherine and frowned. "Is Mom okay?" he asked when she got close enough.

"She and baby Max are just fine."

Relief replaced his frown. "Good. Thank you."

"Of course. Is your dad nearby?"

"He went down to the lodge to deal with that customer who was being such a jerk. He told me come back up here to monitor the slope."

"Okay, thanks." She eyed the path down. It was either walk, or get in her car and drive around. She chose to drive so she could just leave from there.

Katherine took the steps back up to her car, her heart heavy now that she could fully concentrate on finding

Noah. Where was he? And, as much as she didn't want to believe the worst, she couldn't help the niggling of doubt. Was it possible that he'd killed Dominic's partner? Was Noah responsible for breaking into the clinic? The intruder had worn a mask, but he'd been a little on the heavy side, several inches taller than her. The same as Noah. At least, the last that she remembered.

The fact that she was even harboring such thoughts twisted her insides into a tight knot.

She slipped into the driver's seat and turned the key. Nothing.

"Really?" With a sigh, she popped the hood, climbed out and walked around to see if she could figure out what was going on. One of the battery cables was disconnected. She frowned. Weird. She grabbed her toolbox from the back and reconnected the cable, her mind spinning. There was no way that came off all by itself. She heard the footstep behind her, started to turn, only to be stopped by a hand on her arm and something hard jabbed into her rib. "Hey!"

"Shut up and walk or I'll kill you where you stand."

The higher Creed took them up the mountain, the harder Dominic's head throbbed. He'd been fine three thousand feet ago, but he wasn't used to the higher elevation. Especially not with a knock on the skull, but thankfully, it wasn't bad enough to stop him from going with Creed. "So, this guy we're looking for is friends with Noah?"

"I don't know that you'd call them friends at this point in life, but when Noah was here, I vaguely remember him hanging out in the parking lot of the Burnt Burger. A group of teens from the high school met there regularly then. Still do. Same location, mostly different kids."

"She mentioned y'all were looking for them. I didn't have a chance to really ask her about them this morning before she had to take off to the Upworths' place. Wish she'd mentioned them earlier."

"She didn't think about them. *I* didn't think about them until a short time ago. And if Noah didn't talk about them, she wouldn't have known much—if anything— about them. The Burnt Burger is within walking distance of Katherine's home. His last summer here, he was sixteen, close to seventeen. Katherine was working a lot of hours at the clinic, but she never turned down the opportunity to have Noah come stay with her—especially since she missed a lot of his younger years when she was in med school then working her residency."

"I see."

"But I know who the kids are and there are a few who still live in town. The others have gone off to college."

"I'm not worried about the kids who've left. He's looking for someone here. And if that someone isn't Katherine, then it's someone else that he feels like would hide him."

"Exactly." Creed pointed. "That's where Katherine went to deliver Grace's baby."

Dominic could see the snow-covered tubing run. "Looks like a fun place."

"Families love it. They just opened three years ago and have been struggling to stay afloat." He parked. "All of the teens want a job there, of course."

"Of course. Why would you want to bag groceries when you could spend your time at a place like that?"

"Yep. And I happen to know that twenty-one-year-old Gavin McCleary works there part-time. He's also one of the kids Noah used to hang out with."

"Then I can't wait to talk to him." Dominic's phone rang. Leon, his buddy. He swiped the screen. "Hey, Leon."

"I'm just checking in. I wanted to see how you're doing and if you've found Carl's killer yet."

"I'm hanging in there. And no, we haven't found the guy yet. But we will."

"Anything I can do? I can't stand just waiting. I'm not good at waiting."

"Stick to your numbers, my friend. Investment banking is about as treacherous as tracking down killers."

Leon's chuckle sounded forced and Dominic couldn't blame him. No one felt like laughing at the moment. "Are you sure I can't come out there?" Leon asked. "I feel like you need support or something."

Dominic's throat tightened and he cleared it. "You're a good friend, Leon. I appreciate the sentiment. But the best thing you can do right now is pray."

"Yeah. Right. I can do that. Okay, but will you keep me updated? Let me hear from you every now and then to let me know you're okay and what's going on? If you're making any progress?"

"Sure. I can do that."

"Thanks. All right, I've gotta run. I have a client meeting in about ten minutes. Talk to you soon."

They hung up and Dominic swiped a hand over his chin. Creed eyed him. "Good friends are hard to come by. You're a fortunate man."

"I am." He paused. "You and Katherine are close."

"She's one of my best friends."

"And there's nothing…ah…well, you know. You're not interested in…"

"Dating her?"

"Yeah."

"No. She's like a sister. Always has been." He shrugged. "Which is a good thing because if I wanted anything more, she'd break my heart."

Dominic laughed. "I can certainly see how that might happen. Why nothing more? She's a lovely woman with a compassionate heart." Just saying the words made him want to spend more time with her getting to know her.

"Katherine was a hurting teen when she came to stay with my family one year. I know she's told you about her father. He got really bad the year she was fifteen and disappeared for a while. Social services was going to send her off to some home in Asheville. She came to me crying and I couldn't stand it. I asked my parents to let her live with us and they agreed. We grew even closer and she's been my sister ever since." He shrugged. "I just never could see her as anything more."

Dominic heard something behind the words. "Because there's someone else?"

Creed blinked, then chuckled. "Yeah, but I don't talk about it much."

"Why not?"

The sheriff shrugged. "She chose to leave. I chose to stay."

"Gotcha." Silence fell between them for a few seconds before Dominic asked. "You ever think about going after her?"

The sigh from Creed sounded so sad, Dominic wished he'd kept his nosey question to himself.

"I've thought about it, but that was years ago." He

shot Dominic a half smile. "My mom keeps asking me if I'm ever going to settle down. I keep telling her I will when Lacey Lee comes back to town."

"Meaning never?"

"Something like that."

More silence.

"Your mom sounds a lot like mine," Dominic finally said.

"You have any siblings?"

"Yes. I have two sisters. I'm the oldest."

"I would have guessed that."

Dominic laughed. "I'm not sure how to take that."

"No offense. Just type A, driven, successful, bossy." He shrugged. "Makes for a good law officer."

"Well, let's see if you're right and we can boss some answers out of Mr. McCleary."

EIGHT

Katherine had followed the man's instructions to walk and they were still walking, heading behind the run toward the road. The gun was still jammed in her lower back, and his hard grasp clamped on her biceps. Her heart thudded a desperate beat, and her mind whirled with escape scenarios. As a tactical medic, she'd trained for this kind of situation, but now faced with the reality of it—and the fact that she could die should the gun go off—she was scared. Flat-out afraid.

But she'd been afraid before. She could handle this. "Where are you taking me?"

"I've got a car stashed. We're going to get in and take a ride."

"Where?"

"Just shut up and keep walking."

A plan started to take shape, but she needed to act before they got much farther away from the property. Once she was alone with him in his vehicle, her chances of survival diminished exponentially.

However, as long as the gun was pressed against her...

So, she needed it gone.

Now.

Her foot slammed against an exposed root and she went to her knees sinking into the one foot of snow, hands planted on the ground. Her kidnapper gave a surprised grunt and released her. "Get up!"

Katherine pushed herself up and whirled, the edge of her palm slamming against his forearm. Pain radiated from her hand to her shoulder, but the move did what she'd intended. The weapon spun from his grip and he cursed as he dove for it. Katherine bolted back the way they'd come, legs churning. She had a slight head start before hard footsteps pounded behind her. She didn't know if he'd managed to retrieve the gun, but no shots came her way. She pushed hard, her booted feet kicking up the snow.

She made it back to the house, ran down the steps toward the tubing-business parking lot. "I'm going to kill you!"

His words were way too close to her left ear.

Breaths coming in ragged pants, Katherine nevertheless put on a burst of speed, raced past an openmouthed Christopher at the ticket counter and, with a glance back over her shoulder, saw the man chasing her closing in. "Call the cops, Chris!"

With only two other people on the slope, there were plenty of black inner tubes available and several that hadn't been placed back in the rack yet. She grabbed the nearest one and threw herself on it. Her forward momentum sent her speeding down the slick slope.

Cold wind whipped her hair into her face. She spared another quick look back in time to see him pull the same move she had. He was bigger and heavier than she and simple physics said he'd catch up with her before she reached the bottom. Shouts from the top of the run caught her attention, but she had no idea who was yelling or what they were yelling about.

Her focus was on the lodge at the bottom. A patrol car was already there. If she could get inside before the man behind her, she could get help. The end of the run was coming up fast and he was right behind her.

So close she could hear his harsh breaths and muttered threats. She wasn't going to make it to the bottom. His hand swiped out in an attempt to grab her and missed. Barely.

Oh, Lord, please help me. This is going to hurt.

In a quick twist of her upper body, she tipped herself over.

She landed hard in the packed snow. Her teeth snapped together, and she slammed her left shoulder against the ground. She spun and went over the side of the run into a three-foot pile of snow.

The sudden stop stole her breath, but she pushed herself up, and ignored her throbbing shoulder and aching lungs, to search for her would-be kidnapper.

People stared, and the run patrol aimed their skis her way. Where was he?

Movement to her left swiveled her attention in that direction. "Get down! He's got a gun!"

Screams echoed. A figure rose, stared at her through the slit in his mask from his landing spot ten feet away. He lifted his hand and aimed his weapon at her. This time she noted the suppressor on the end.

Katherine shot from her crouched position and ran to the nearest tree, gasping when pain arched through her shoulder and into her neck.

She waited for the gunshot. When it didn't come, she

sucked in a breath and tried to listen over the pounding of her heart.

Had the cops seen them? She reached into the pocket of her vest and closed her fingers around her phone.

Underbrush snapped behind her sending her scurrying to the next large tree in search of cover. She crouched next to it, then tapped the screen of her phone, found Creed's number and dialed it.

She hung up after the third ring and texted him. In trouble. Need help. At the run.

Katherine made sure her ringer was off, attached her location and hit Send. Blood pounded through her veins, but she had her breathing under control. In through her nose, out through her mouth. Silent and steady.

Come on, Creed, answer your phone.

Silence.

She hated to do it, but if Creed wasn't going to answer…she shot the same text to Dominic, Regina and Ben. Then attached her location. Surely one of them would see her message.

Two seconds later, her phone vibrated with a text from Creed. We're on the way. What's going on?

Man with a gun chasing me. I can't move without giving away my hiding spot.

Stay put. I'll let Ben and Regina know.

Once again, she heard her pursuer nearby and kept as still as possible.

A low curse reached her from the other side of the large trees. "I can't find her. Yeah. Yeah. I'm getting out of here. The cops are headed this way, and I've got to hide the car. There'll be another opportunity."

Another opportunity? Why were they trying to grab her? It was Dominic that they wanted. Wasn't it?

His footsteps carried him away from her and Katherine let out a low breath, her adrenaline dropping, making her feel light-headed and weak.

"Katherine?" She recognized Regina's voice. "Katherine? Are you out here?"

"Yes! I'm coming, but be careful. The guy has a gun with a suppressor on it." With one final look in the direction she'd last heard him, Katherine pushed herself to her feet, stepped out of her hiding spot and ran toward her friend. Regina pulled her behind her and swept her weapon in the direction Katherine had come from. "I think he's gone," Katherine said, her breath hitching. "I heard him on the phone with someone. He said he had to get the car."

Ben got on his radio. "Need a unit to Holloway Road. Looking for a car parked with easy access to Upworth's Tubing though the woods." Confirmation of a unit on the way came through the speaker and Ben nodded. "I'll see what I can find."

He took off and Regina gestured toward the lodge. "Come on, let's get you in front of the fire so you can thaw out and fill us in. Creed and Dominic are here, too."

"That fast?" Katherine hadn't realized how cold she was until Regina mentioned it. She shivered and tugged her coat tighter under her chin.

"They were close by, following a lead on Noah."

"What lead?"

"Gavin McCleary."

Katherine blinked. "Gavin? He knows Noah?"

"Apparently. I'll let Creed fill you in."

"Okay. Thanks." Now she really wanted to get to the lodge.

Regina's phone pinged, and she glanced at it with a low groan.

"What is it?" Katherine asked.

"Nothing work related. It's Mom. My sister's with her. Lisa says Mom fell. She's bruised, but nothing's broken."

"Oh, no! I'm so sorry. Do you want me to go with you to check on her?"

"No, Lisa's got it covered. She was just letting me know. I'll deal with that later. Come on—let's get you warmed up."

While Ben went after her attacker, she followed Regina through the snow, rubbing her throbbing shoulder. Carefully, she rotated it and breathed a relieved sigh when it was only sore. Nothing broken or sprained.

Regina pushed open the lodge door and Katherine stepped inside, relishing the instant heat that hit her.

"Katherine." Dominic strode toward her and took her chilled hands in his. "Are you all right?"

More warmth flooded her at his concern. His blue eyes locked on hers and her heart did a funny tremble at the look. He cared. She cleared her throat. "I'm fine." She'd been taking care of herself and everyone else for so long, she wasn't sure how to process his worry. Katherine pulled her hands from his and shoved them into her vest pockets.

A flicker of hurt crossed his face before he hid it behind a smooth facade. Guilt hit her, and she made a mental note to apologize to him when they were alone.

But she also reminded herself that this was the man who had tried and found Noah guilty before he knew the whole story. She turned to Creed. "That guy was after me for some reason."

"Did he say why?"

"No. He didn't say much of anything except to order me to shut up and walk." She paused. "Then when I overheard him on the phone, he said that he couldn't find her and that he had to get out of there because the cops were on the way. And that there'd be another opportunity."

"Another opportunity for what?"

"It sounded like another opportunity...to grab me."

Dominic blinked. "To grab you? Why would anyone want to kidnap you?"

"Trust me, that question has been first and foremost in my mind since I overheard him."

"You think he thought he could use you to get to Dominic? Or Noah?" Creed asked.

"I think that's probably the most logical assumption. Before you showed up yesterday—and before Noah pulled his disappearing act—I haven't had a hint of trouble." Dominic winced and she shot him a sympathetic look. "No offense."

"None taken."

"But there have definitely been no kidnapping attempts. However, if they were trying to get to Dominic or Noah via me, and they've been watching, they would have known Dominic was at the clinic." She shrugged. "They might have even figured out he was staying with me. If it was someone after Noah... I don't know."

"That all makes sense," Dominic said. "I'm really sorry."

"Well, now that we know how far they're willing to go," Creed said, "we can take precautions."

Dominic nodded. "I'll get a hotel room and make sure I'm very visible doing it."

Creed shook his head. "That's not what I'm thinking. I'm not sure getting a hotel will work at this point. If they think snatching Katherine will entice you to trade yourself for her then I don't see separating you two to be the answer. I think you should stay together so it's easier for my small department to protect you."

"I can call in a few friends, as well," Dominic said, his tone wry. "I do have some very well-trained connections."

Creed smirked. "The ones who let Noah get away?"

Dominic grimaced. "Touché."

"I'm kidding." Creed's brief flash of humor turned serious. "I think having a few marshals scattered around the area might not be a bad thing, but the truth is, you can't hide forever and these people may be willing to just bide their time and wait until things settle down before they strike again."

"Maybe," Katherine said. "In the meantime, while we're waiting for things to calm down, I'd like to head back home and finish some paperwork."

"I thought you had the next few days off," Dominic said.

"Hm, so did I." She flashed him a quick grin, revealing a shallow dimple in her left cheek.

"Come on, you two," Creed said, "I'll follow you home, then I'll—"

"Oh, wait," Katherine said. "What did you find out

about Gavin McCleary? I didn't realize he and Noah were that close."

"We didn't get a chance to talk to him before we had to run over here and rescue you," Creed said.

Katherine scowled. "I kind of rescued myself, thank you very much." Then her features softened. "But I appreciate how fast you got here. Why don't we go to Gavin's and see what he knows before we head back to my place?"

"We?" Dominic asked.

She shrugged. "I want to know what he says. There's another guy we can talk to, as well. He's Grace and Mark Upworth's nephew. Patrick Taylor."

Creed nodded. "Yeah, you mentioned him. Patrick and Gavin are good buddies."

Katherine pinched the bridge of her nose and shook her head. "I can't believe I was so oblivious as to who Noah was hanging out with." She sighed. "It wasn't intentional."

"It's not your fault," Dominic said. "You're not his parent in spite of the fact that it sounds like you've tried to be the mother figure in his life."

"I know that. At least my head does, but when I let him come stay with me, I was taking on that responsibility, and it doesn't seem like I did a very good job."

Dominic could tell she was going to carry that burden and nothing he said was going to convince her otherwise. "Did you teach him right from wrong?" he asked, unable to totally give up trying.

"Of course."

"Then you did your part. More than your part, if you ask me. I got to know Noah a little bit when we were transporting him to different places. Mostly safe houses, a couple of doctor's appointments, that kind of thing. He's a bright kid and seemed to be serious about wanting to turn his life around after testifying. Which is why I was shocked when pulled his Houdini routine. But, before all that, he mentioned you a few times."

Katherine's eyes widened. "He did?"

"Yeah. He said he had to get himself straightened out. That you'd be disappointed in him."

Tears glinted for a brief second before she looked away. "Thank you for telling me that. I wasn't sure he cared what I thought anymore."

"He cares. At least I thought he did. Now, I'm not so sure what was going through his head."

"He's scared," she said. "Something spooked him big-time for him to do this."

"Maybe." He glanced at Creed. "Katherine and I can follow you back to Gavin's if that's all right."

"Sure." Creed looked at Katherine. "But you stay in the car."

"Fine. As long as you tell me everything." At his raised brow, she cleared her throat. "Okay, fine. Everything you legally can."

"Of course."

"Then I'm ready when y'all are," Katherine said.

"Come on—I'll give you a ride back to your car."

Once he was seated in the passenger seat and Katherine behind the wheel, he buckled his seat belt and studied her as she pulled out of the Upworths' drive. "Are you sure you're all right?"

She swallowed and gave a small shrug without taking her eyes from the road. "I'm a little embarrassed to say I'm shaken, but I'll be okay."

"Shaken is nothing to be ashamed of. Not after that kind of experience."

"I know, but I've been trained to take care of myself and he completely surprised me."

"Don't beat yourself up, Katherine. No one could have seen that coming."

She shot him a sideways glance and bobbed a short nod. "Again, I know, but thank you for trying to help."

"Trying and failing?" he asked.

She laughed. "Yes, but it's the effort that counts. At least in this case."

"Tell me about your tactical medic days, if you don't mind."

"Those were some good days. I worked with the Atlanta, Georgia, SWAT team for four years before transferring to a hospital. When I got tired of working twenty-four seven in what I call hit-and-run medicine, I decided to move home to Timber Creek. Best thing I could have done for my peace of mind in some ways. Other ways, it's made my life more stressful."

"How so?"

"I'm closer to my dad now and see him more often. Which is good because I can provide some things he needs, but it's also frustrating, too, because I can't convince him to come home. He has a perfectly good house sitting there, waiting for him, and he continues to stay on the streets. It makes me mad and sad and…everything else."

"I'm sorry."

"Me, too." She shrugged. "All I can do is keep trying."

"Does anyone ever take care of you?"

She let out a low laugh. "Take care of me?" A soft smile curved her lips. "Yeah. Buddy does. He's my emotional-support dog in some ways. Or he would be, if he was mine."

"He's yours."

Another laugh slipped from her, and Dominic's heart lightened. He liked hearing her laugh. Liked being the one to make her laugh.

"What about you?"

"What about me?"

"Have you always wanted to be a marshal?"

"Yep. Ever since I can remember. I saw a movie once about a marshal chasing a fugitive who was framed for killing his wife. All the guy wanted to do was clear his name. All the marshal wanted to do was bring the guy in."

"Hm. I remember that movie. Turns out the fugitive was innocent."

Dominic gave a short chuckle and shook his head. "Yes. Yes, he was. But that is fiction. I haven't chased an innocent man yet."

"There's always a first time."

He fell silent and five minutes later she pulled to the curb of the log-cabin-style home. The house sat on the side of the hill overlooking the winding road that would eventually lead them back to town.

Katherine put the Subaru in Park and sat back in the seat. Dominic opened his door and stepped out. He turned back to her. "Keep the doors locked, would you? For my peace of mind?"

"Of course."

"And lay on the horn if you see anything weird."

"Like a man with a gun?"

"Like that."

"I'll be fine." She shooed him toward the house. "Now go see if Gavin knows where Noah is."

"Yes, ma'am."

He shut the door and she hit the power locks. Her gaze met his and he stood for a moment, heart tugging with an emotion he'd not felt in a very long time.

He cleared his throat and gave her a little wave. She returned it and he spun to catch up with Creed who stood on the porch watching him with a raised brow.

Dominic ignored the man's thinly veiled amusement.

"She's a special one," Creed said. "Be careful."

"I don't know what you're talking about." He kept his voice even, his tone mild.

"Right."

Creed knocked, and Dominic couldn't help shooting a glance back at the woman in the car.

She was special for sure—but was she hiding something about a potential killer?

He didn't think so, but he'd been wrong before.

NINE

Dominic and Creed stood on the front porch, waiting for someone to answer the door. Katherine closed her eyes and pinched the bridge of her nose. A headache had started pounding in her temples and she wanted nothing more than to go home and have a hot soak in her oversize tub.

But she opened her eyes to the reality that Noah was out there somewhere. Running scared. Lost. Alone. Maybe needing her. Definitely in trouble. In spite of Dominic's pretty words, Katherine knew she'd failed Noah when he'd been a teen. Now she had to find him and make it right.

Please, God, keep him safe and help me find him before anyone else does.

The door opened, and Katherine recognized Gavin's mother. Creed said something and the woman frowned, shaking her head. She shut the door and Katherine rolled her window down. Before she could ask what was going on, the door opened again and Gavin joined the two men on the porch. He had on fleece pajama bottoms, a hoodie and flip-flops. Katherine refused to tell him to go put some socks on before he wound up in her clinic with pneumonia.

"Mom said you wanted to ask me about Noah Bennett?" the twenty-year-old said. He raked a hand through his bed-head hair, causing it to spike even more.

"I'm US Marshal Dominic O'Ryan. I guess you've seen the news?"

"Of course. It's all anyone's talking about right now." He crossed his arms and jutted his chin. "And I don't believe a word of it. That's so wrong. Noah wouldn't do what they're saying."

"We don't know if he would or not," Creed said, "which is why we need to find him. Have you seen him?"

"No." He shrugged. "I haven't heard from him in about a year or so."

"Any idea where he'd head if he was coming this way?"

Gavin ran a hand over his head once more. "No. Maybe to see his sister, but even that's just a guess. Last time I talked to Noah, he said she'd done something to make him mad so they weren't on speaking terms."

Katherine flinched. What in the world had she done to make him mad?

She pulled her phone from her purse and dialed her mother's number.

"Hello?"

"Hi, Mom."

"Oh, I thought you might be Noah."

Katherine tried not to let the obvious disappointment sting, but it wasn't easy. "You didn't recognize my number?"

"I didn't look at the number. I just answered it."

Right. "I take it you haven't heard from him."

"No. Why does everyone keep asking? I haven't seen

or heard from him in months. Just like I told the marshals who came to the house."

Katherine rubbed her eyes. "Okay, then do you have any idea why he'd run to Timber Creek?"

"No. Unless he was running to see you."

"I haven't spoken to him in three years, Mom. Why would he all of a sudden run to me?"

Her mother fell silent.

"Mom?"

"I don't know. All I know is for the past three years, he's been nothing but trouble. If you see him, tell him not to bother coming home."

Click.

Katherine blinked. She shuddered and simply stared at her phone. The knock on the passenger window jerked her out of her stupor. She hit the button to unlock the door. Dominic opened it and slid into the seat. "Katherine? You okay?"

Dominic slid into the seat. "Katherine? You okay?"

She pulled in a deep breath and looked up at him. "Um…yes. Yes, I'm fine. Did you learn anything?"

"Not from Gavin. My gut tells me he doesn't know where Noah is."

She nodded. She hadn't really thought he would and hadn't gotten her hopes up. But they'd had to try. She honed in on Dominic's pale face. "Your head is hurting, isn't it?"

Her shot her a strained smile. "A bit."

"I suspect that's an understatement. There's a bottle of ibuprofen in the glove box. Help yourself." He did and she waved to Creed, who stopped at her window. "What's next?"

"Patrick's working at the garage in town. I'll follow

you two back to your place so the superhero here can crash before his head explodes."

She thought she heard Dominic cover a low chuckle by clearing his throat. "Banged your head before, have you?"

"A time or two." Creed turned his attention back to her. "Take it slow. I'll be right behind you."

"Thanks, Creed."

He nodded and headed to his cruiser.

"Well, Mr. Superhero," Katherine said with a smirk, "buckle up."

"I'm no superhero," he said, his voice soft. "If I was, I could have stopped my partner from getting shot and killed."

She reached over and gripped his hand. His fingers curled around hers and shivers skated up her arm. "I'm really sorry," she said.

He nodded. "I know." His phone rang and he snagged it from his pocket. "Sorry, I need to get this."

"Of course."

"Hello?"

Katherine put the car in gear and pulled away from the curb. Creed followed her two car lengths behind and she found she was glad for his presence. The attack at the Upworth property had done more than shaken her. It had terrified her and left her unable to think about much of anything else.

"You're where?" His question echoed through the car and Katherine jerked her attention to him. "No, it's fine. I'm just working a case and won't have time—" He listened. "Okay. Sure. Thanks. I'll see you in a little bit." He hung up and sighed.

"Wanna share?"

He rubbed his eyes then glanced at her. "That was my buddy, Evan Kennedy. He just pulled into town and checked in at the hotel."

"To support you?"

"Yes. Unfortunately, I won't have a lot of time for socializing with him."

"Surely, he understands that."

"He does, but I'll still feel weird. I don't want to blow him off, but since I can't investigate Carl's shooting, my first priority is finding Noah."

She could relate. "But you think he shot Carl."

His jaw tightened then relaxed. "I don't know if he did or not. He's the only suspect we have, and his actions shout guilt."

"Or fear," she said. While she kept her voice soft, her fingers flexed around the wheel.

To his credit, Dominic didn't immediately discount her statement. Instead, he simply nodded. "Then we need to find him and ask him."

Katherine shot him a glance. "Why are you so sure that I'm wrong about Noah?"

He rubbed his jaw. "I'm sure you think you're right. I even understand that you want to believe he's innocent—"

"At least until he's proven…not. Wouldn't you feel the same way if it was your brother?"

"Probably. But I can't…"

"Can't what?"

"Take your word for it."

"Well…I guess I can understand that." She went silent for a moment while she watched the trees pass on her left. She hugged the double yellow line as she took each curve, keeping her speed at a rate that wouldn't cause Creed to yell at her when they stopped. She liked to drive fast, but not on mountain roads. "I'm sure you have guilty people," she said, "and their relatives protest their innocence all the time."

"I do. And so did my dad. He believed the woman who hysterically insisted that her husband was innocent of murdering his two friends, and when he went to talk to him, the man shot him."

She gasped.

"So," he said, "you might call me a little skeptical when others promise their loved ones are innocent."

When Katherine fell silent, Dominic knew he'd hit a nerve, but he had to make her understand that he wasn't judging Noah's guilt or innocence based on a whim.

Dominic's father had learned a hard lesson in realizing there were some very skilled actors and actresses in the crime arena. Dominic didn't need to learn that lesson personally. He'd learned it while he watched his father try to learn to walk again. He'd learned it while he listened to his dad beat himself up over being too trusting and gullible. Bitterness had set in and while Dominic had tried hard not to let it affect him, he'd be the first to admit some of it had rubbed off.

Hence his inability to shake his skepticism—or the swirling pity that she was so blind to her brother's guilt. He hated that he was going to be the one to expose the young man for what he really was.

A criminal and a killer.

Or was he? He couldn't help the small voice that popped into his head. Everything he'd told her about Noah had been true. And recounting her brother's desire to do the right thing and do something with his life echoed in his mind. What if she was right? What if Noah was running out of fear, not guilt?

But what had made him so afraid that he'd risk losing everything to run?

Dominic stole another look at Katherine's tense profile. She wasn't stupid. And she didn't come across as being in denial about her brother's criminal activities related to his involvement with organized crime. So, why was she so sure that he hadn't been the one who'd pulled the trigger and killed Carl?

He shook his head. She simply had to be blinded by her love for her brother. And Dominic couldn't let his growing feelings for her sway his own beliefs. Noah was guilty. Period.

"Tell me about your friend," she said. "His name is Evan?"

He breathed a silent relieved sigh at a question that was free of conflict. "Yeah. We've been friends since middle school. He and Leon and I were known as the three amigos and were inseparable all the way through high school. Leon and I even went to the same college, but Evan wound up at Harvard."

"Oh, my. Impressive."

"Evan's an impressive kind of guy. He graduated at the top of his class and could have done pretty much anything he wanted, but, to his parents' mortification, became a mere college professor." He wiggled the air quotes around the three words. "His parents' description, not his or anyone else's who knows him."

"He loves it, right?"

"He's in his element. Loves teaching."

"He's also a good friend if he'd come all this way to check on you."

Dominic nodded. "He and Carl hit it off the minute I introduced them five years ago. Leon, too, but Carl and Evan especially. They'd hang out even when I wasn't around." He laughed. "At first, it kind of bothered me, but I got over it." He sobered. "They've been great friends. I don't know how we're going to manage without Carl."

A loud crash from behind jerked Dominic around in time to see the sheriff's vehicle go over the side of the mountain. "Creed!"

"What happened?" Katherine slammed on the brakes and pulled to the shoulder, gravel crunching under her tires. Her gaze swung to his, eyes wide. "What happened?"

"Creed went off the mountain."

Shock flashed briefly. "But…why?"

The back window shattered, and they ducked. "I think it's an ambush."

He barely got the sentence out of his mouth when two more bullets pinged off the side of the car.

Dominic yanked his phone from his pocket and dialed 911, then tapped the button to put it on speaker. With narrowed eyes, Katherine opened the glove compartment and pulled out a weapon just as the dispatcher came on the line.

"What's your emergency?" The woman's voice came through soothing and confident.

He rattled off the information. "Officer in need of assistance. He went over the edge of the mountain." He shot another glance at Katherine. "What's our location?"

"Susan, this is Katherine. We're at the curve just past the old mill on Highway 217."

"Katherine? You okay?"

"We are, but Creed's in trouble and I'm not sure I can get to him with someone shooting at us."

"Shooting at—never mind. I've got help coming. Stay on the line with me."

Bullets slammed into the back of the Subaru and he heard Susan's gasp. "Katherine?"

"We're okay, but tell them to hurry!"

When Dominic focused back on Katherine, she'd turned to examine the area where he'd seen Creed go over. "You okay with fighting back?" he asked.

"I don't want either of us to get shot or have to shoot anyone," she said, "but I'm not leaving here without Creed." And they both knew that might mean shooting back. If they could spot a target.

"I'm with you," he said.

"Susan, we're going to try to get to Creed."

"Be careful."

"The bullets are coming from behind us," Katherine told him. "We can't do anything in this position."

"I agree. What do you have in mind?"

Her answer was to step on the gas, spin the wheel to the left for a tight, turn then she aimed her car for the shoulder of the oncoming traffic lane, pulling close to where Creed had gone down. So far no one else had come by, but that wouldn't last forever. Officers would block the traffic in both directions now that they knew the location and that there was an active shooter.

They tumbled from her Subaru and bullets kicked up the gravel around Dominic. He ducked behind the open passenger door, weapon in his hand. "Stay low!"

More bullets pounded the ground and shattered the window of the passenger side. Glass rained down around him and he peered around the edge of the door, searching for the shooter.

"I need to get to Creed!"

Katherine's shout came from the rear of the vehicle. He knew immediately what she planned to do. She was going to try to bolt down the side of the mountain. "Don't do it, Katherine! I don't know where the shooter is, and you'll be exposed." For now, the shooting had stopped, and the faint sound of sirens reached him. "Help is coming. Just stay put!"

She slipped up beside him. "I have to help him," she said, her breath coming in quick pants. "Seconds could matter in whether or not he lives or dies."

"And if you get shot because the shooter can see you, that's not going to help anyone."

Her struggle was reflected in her gaze. "I know, but…" She spun. "Get in the car. You drive."

"What?"

"Pull down farther so that I can get out and see where he is. Use this big tank as cover."

While it was risky, it might work. And Creed's life— if he was still alive—might depend on it. "Let me go down."

"Where'd you get your medical degree?"

"Right." Another bullet hit the hood, and Dominic dove into the passenger seat then maneuvered around so he was able to crawl feetfirst into the driver's. Thankfully, Katherine was a tall woman who drove with the seat pushed back and he was able to shimmy into it while keeping his head down. Katherine slid into the passenger seat. "Go, please. Hang on, Creed," she whispered.

"Stay low."

He pressed the gas and inched forward, the tires crunching on the gravel.

A sharp crack reached him just before the driver's-side mirror disappeared. Dominic flinched, but arrived to the spot where Creed's car had gone down.

Katherine reached into the back seat to grab her medical bag, then opened her door and tumbled out.

TEN

"You see him?"

Dominic's shout came over the wail of the sirens that were practically on top of them at this point.

"Not yet!" Katherine examined the broken limbs and crushed vegetation. The mountain was steep, but not impossible to inch her way down, using the trees to keep her balance. While grateful for her all-terrain boots, she wished she'd grabbed her gloves. But getting to Creed fast was her priority. Smoke curled from below, blocking most of her view, but she could make out Creed's cruiser wedged up against a cluster of trees. It was driver's-side down.

"Creed!" Her foot hit a patch of slick leaves, and she went down hard. "Oof." She slid ten feet before she was able to snag a jutting root and halt her descent. In the process, her arm scraped across something and a lightening flash of pain arched through her. She ignored it, her attention focused on getting to the cruiser. "Creed!"

No more shots sounded, but the sirens from Creed's cruiser had stopped. She couldn't see the edge of the road from her vantage point. However, since no more gunshots rang through the air, she could only hope the shooter was gone.

"Katherine!"

She looked up to see Dominic making his way down. "No, Dominic. Don't come down! Let rescue do that!" The last he needed was to hit his head again.

He ignored her. "Of course," she muttered. Then focused on reaching the patrol vehicle. "Creed! Answer me!" *Please, be able to answer me.*

Katherine finally reached the SUV, noting the smoking had mostly stopped.

A rough cough came from the interior, and she nearly wilted with relief. "Creed! Are you okay?"

"Yeah!" More coughing. "I'm all right. I think. Banged up, but I'm breathing."

A bloody hand appeared through the broken passenger window and he grabbed hold to pull himself up. His head popped through and she could make out a gash at his hairline. Blood dripped from his jaw, but his dark eyes caught hers. He pulled one more time and got his upper torso out of the window. The cruiser shifted, creaking and groaning.

"Creed! Stop! Don't move!"

He froze, halfway in the vehicle, halfway out. Katherine looked back to see Dominic closing in. "I need a rope or something. We have to get him out before the car falls!"

Dominic stopped his downward climb, reversed his steps a few yards and looked up. "Throw me a rope!" She couldn't see whoever he was yelling at, but apparently he was satisfied someone heard him.

"Wait on rescue," Creed hollered at her. "Don't come any closer." The car let out a long squeal as it tilted, rocking across the thick trunk. Creed closed his eyes and the vehicle finally stilled. For the moment.

"There's no time to wait. Tell them to hurry, Dominic!" She looked back at Creed and his gaze locked on hers. "Hold on, Creed." She moved closer, inching her way toward him. Debris rolled under her feet and splashed down on the rear passenger door.

"Don't do it, Katherine," Creed said. "It's too dangerous."

"Yes, well, since when have I ever played it safe?"

"Katherine!"

She turned at Dominic's shout and he tossed her the end of a rope, already looped on both ends. She snagged it midair and swung back to Creed. "If I toss this to you, can you somehow manage to get it around you?"

"You can't hold me."

"I'll hold you." She stepped into one loop and pulled up around her waist. Then, moving sideways, she worked her way around a tree trunk to give her some leverage. "Ready?"

"Ready."

She tossed the loop to Creed who caught it. The cruiser tilted and slid to the left before the back end hit the ground and stopped with a shudder. Creed, still propped on the passenger door, flipped the rope around his head and quickly maneuvered one arm through the loop.

The cruiser gave one last death groan, scraped off the trunk of the tree and slid down the side of the steeper part of the mountain. Creed disappeared over the ledge.

"Creed! No!"

The rope went taut around her waist and yanked her to the ground with a hard slam. The breath whooshed from her lungs and she gasped.

Dimly, she heard Dominic yelling at her. The rope bit into her even through the protective layer of her heavy coat. She ignored it and focused on scrambling for a way to resist the weight that wanted to pull her toward the ledge and over the side after Creed. Without the tree, she never would have had a chance.

The pressure around her waist lessened. She took advantage of the reprieve to drag in a ragged breath.

"Walk backward, Katherine."

Dominic's words spurred her. She looked over her shoulder to see him standing braced against a tree trunk, rope wrapped around him. "I've got you, but you're going to have to help."

Adrenaline fired through her and with both hands gripping the thick twine and Dominic pulling behind her, she was able to place one foot behind the other.

Step after step. "Don't stop," Dominic said. "Keep going."

Was Creed on the other end of the rope? He had to be. It was too hard to move for him not to be. And yet, the fact that she was even *able* to move worried her.

No, he must be helping by pulling himself up with each step she took back.

Seconds later, his head appeared, and his hands grabbed at the ground. Katherine wasn't sure how he did it, but he'd somehow pushed his way free of the falling vehicle. She wanted to cry. Instead, she gritted her teeth and bent her knees. Her muscles quivered, but she dug in and continued her backward pace.

Until, finally, Creed was up and over the ledge and lying on the ground. The rope loosened and she dropped to her knees.

Creed pushed himself up on his elbows and army

crawled away from the edge. Katherine forced herself to her feet, ignored her trembling, overworked muscles and hurried to her friend's side. Dominic joined her. In the chaos, she had lost her medical bag, so she could only pray Creed didn't need anything in it.

"Creed," she whispered, placing a hand on his shoulder. He groaned. "Lie still. Help is at the top."

"The shooter," he rasped.

"Gone as far as we can tell."

Dominic nodded. His face was pale and a vein throbbed in his temple. After that exertion, his head had to be killing him. But she and Creed would both be at the bottom of the mountain without him. She caught his eye. "Thank you," she said.

"Yeah. How is he?"

"I can hear you, dude," Creed said.

"Very glad of that."

"Anything hurt?" she asked.

"Just about everything. I had my seat belt on but got tossed around pretty good."

Katherine ran professional hands over the sheriff's extremities. "I don't think anything's broken."

She pressed on his abdomen below his rib cage on the left side and he hissed a pained breath. "Think you found something, Doc."

"I think I did. Pretty sure it's your spleen."

"Ruptured?"

"Not sure yet." She glanced up the mountain and cringed at the thought of trying to climb it with a wounded man. She turned to Dominic. "They're coming down, right?"

"Yeah."

"Creed's going to need a basket to haul him up."

Dominic nodded and barely hid a wince.

Make that two wounded men.

"I don't need a basket," Creed said. He started to push to his feet and promptly went back down again.

Katherine gripped his biceps. What was it with these men? "Not smart, my friend."

"I just figured that out."

"Hold on!" a voice shouted from the top. "We're coming!"

Forty-five minutes later, Creed was in the ambulance and Katherine was examining her demolished vehicle.

Dominic stepped up beside her. "I'm sorry."

"It's not your fault. I'll get a rental while the insurance adjuster figures out what to do with this." She paused. "Is bullet-hole damage covered?"

"I have no idea."

A deep sigh welled up within her and filtered through her lips. "Well, I guess I'll deal with that later. I need to get that rental, then I want to get to the hospital to check on Creed."

Before he could respond, a cruiser pulled to a stop, and Ben Land climbed out. "Creed said y'all needed some police protection."

"You sure you want to risk it since you saw how well that worked out for Creed?" Katherine asked.

He shot her a small smile. "I knew what I signed up for when I went to the academy. Let's get you home."

"I'd rather head to the hospital to check on Creed."

"He said not to let you come. In fact, he said if I allowed you to do so, I was fired."

Katherine gaped. "What? He can't do that."

"He's the sheriff—I reckon he can do what he wants."

Creed would no more fire Ben than he'd hop on a

spaceship to the moon. In fact space travel would be more likely. But she got the point.

"Seriously," Ben said. "Creed's fine, but he's worried about you two. Said as long as you were holed up at your place with me on the door, he could rest easier." A pause. "And to remind you that he's wounded, headed for surgery to remove his spleen and needs his rest."

"So, he's not above a guilt trip," Katherine murmured.

"Not at all."

What could she say to that? "Fine."

He motioned for them to climb inside the cruiser. "We've got marshals and state police combing this area for the shooter and your brother. Something's bound to turn up in the next few hours."

Katherine buckled her seat belt and rested her head against the back of the seat, noting that her right arm was throbbing in time with the beat of her heart. She'd check it when she got home. Right now, she was too worn out. And scared to death for her brother.

Oh, Noah, what have you gotten mixed up in?

Because while she really couldn't believe he was the one shooting at her and Dominic or was responsible for sending Creed down the mountain, he was involved somehow. But he wasn't a murderer.

But then again, what did she know?

Dominic's head still pounded, and his waist was bruised from the pull of the rope. His hands had fared slightly better as he'd pulled on his gloves. But he'd admit the headache was about to do him in. Nausea swirled and he finally caved and took the pain pill Katherine wordlessly handed to him.

"Thanks."

"I can tell you're miserable."

"A bit."

"I know I said so before, but thank you for saving our lives." She drew in a breath. "I probably shouldn't have gone down the mountain, but if I hadn't…and if you hadn't…"

"Yeah. It all worked out in the end. That's the important thing to focus on."

"That's what I keep telling myself."

He hesitated and closed his eyes until he felt the pill start to work. When he lifted his lids, Katherine was still there, watching him. The compassion in her gaze sent his heart pounding. He cleared his throat. "We still need to talk to that young man you know. The one who hung around with Gavin and Noah."

"Patrick."

He nodded and instantly regretted it when the stabbing pain nearly drove him to the floor. "I think I'm going to lie down. Maybe Beth and Owen can talk to Patrick."

"I think that might be a wise move."

He'd just made himself comfortable on the couch when a noise from the kitchen sent tension threading through him and he stiffened.

Katherine rested a hand on his arm. "It's just Buddy. I recognize the sound of the doggy door opening and closing."

Dominic grunted. "He's probably hungry. Make sure he doesn't think you're lunch."

She huffed a short laugh. "Buddy's a marshmallow…"

Not exactly how Dominic would describe him.

"…as long as you don't do anything to send him into protection mode."

That was more along the lines of what he was thinking. She rose and he noted the blood-soaked sleeve on her forearm. "Hey, you're hurt." He sat back up, relieved when his head didn't start the ferocious pounding again. It felt a little floaty thanks to the narcotic, but he could deal with that.

She glanced at her arm. "Yes. I didn't notice it until we were in the car on the way here. My coat soaked up most of the blood, but I guess I need to clean it up. Are you okay for a little bit?"

"Sure."

She left and Dominic closed his eyes. Then opened them. She was right-handed and the cut was on her right forearm. He rose and stood for a moment to make sure he was going to be steady on his feet, then headed to the bathroom.

Buddy watched him from the kitchen entrance. "I'm just going to help her out, okay?"

The dog tilted his massive head then turned and padded to the dish that was always full.

In spite of the initial acceptance when he'd first arrived, Dominic hadn't been sure that the dog was okay with him being there. Feeling like he'd passed some kind of test known only to the canine, Dominic walked down the hall to the bathroom. The door was open wide enough to see Katherine sitting on the side of the tub, right arm propped on her thigh, left hand working to saturate the material of her sleeve with water in order to pull it from the wound. Dominic rapped his knuckles on the door and she looked up. "What's wrong?" she asked.

"Nothing, other than that I should have offered to

help you." He took the cloth from her hand and palmed her slender arm.

"I can do it," she said. "I know your head feels like it's going to come off your shoulders."

"Not quite that bad at the moment and I want to help."

"Dominic—"

"Please? You've gone above and beyond for me. I need to do this for you."

She studied him, her gaze serious and curious. "Okay."

He assessed the damage. "Looks like you bled quite a bit."

"I think a sharp branch or a piece of metal from the car got me. Not really sure."

"I'm assuming you're up-to-date on your shots?"

"Of course."

The amusement in her voice almost made him smile. Instead, he frowned. "Doesn't it hurt?"

"Yes."

He frowned. "But you made sure I was settled, and Buddy was taken care of and you weren't going to ask for help." A statement, not a question.

"No, didn't really think about it."

"Do you ever ask for help?"

"Sure, when I need it."

Which was never? "When's the last time you needed it?"

She huffed a sigh and a short laugh. "Um… I don't know." She fell silent for a moment, then shrugged. "Stop looking at me like that. I know it's an issue I need to work on. But the truth is, I asked my dad for help a few times and after he said he would, he didn't.

I learned early on that if I wanted something done, it was better to just do it myself."

"That stinks."

"I know."

"I'm sorry." He ran more water over the cloth then pressed it back to her arm. "Have you talked to him lately?"

"I've tried, but he's not answering his phone. I need to go down there and look for him."

"But I've kept you from doing so, haven't I?"

"Well, not just you. I need to feel like I'm doing something to help find Noah. He's the priority right now. Dad can wait."

"Tell me about him."

"Before Mom left us, he was a good dad. I have some really sweet memories of hanging out with him, watching movies, grabbing ice cream at the general store, going hiking and working in his workshop, but after Mom took off, he just…shattered into a million pieces. And nothing I did was enough for him to want to put the pieces back together."

"That wasn't on you, Katherine."

She smiled. A soft sad smile that went straight to his heart. "I know. At least I know that now. Anyway, I've tried to get him to come home, but he won't," she said, her words low and tight. "His house is sitting there empty. He has a place to live. I even made sure the HVAC system was working and the water and power are on. All of his woodworking tools are cleaned and in working order. All he has to do is come home." She gave a slight shrug. "But he won't for whatever reason."

"Does he have mental health problems?"

"I think he's depressed. So deeply depressed that he

can't see there's a way out. That help is waiting on him, that I've got my hand out and all he has to do is grab it. And I don't know how to make him see it."

"That's hard."

"It is."

He hesitated then said, "Not everyone is the same, of course, and people wind up on the streets for a multitude of reasons, but there *are* some people who choose that life because it's easier than reality."

"I know. But his crash when my mom left us was so hard, I don't know how to describe it. He turned to alcohol for comfort and I…well, like I said, I tried to help, but didn't know how."

"No other relatives?"

"My mom's sister lives in Nevada somewhere. My grandparents are there, as well. Once Mom left, I never heard from any of them again."

The sleeve finally released its grip on the wound allowing the blood to flow freely once more. He pressed the wet cloth to it then released it to get a good look. Katherine got one, too, and grimaced.

"You probably could use a couple of stitches in that," he said.

"Probably."

He grabbed a packet of the gauze she'd set on the floor, opened it and placed it on her arm. "Finish telling me."

"There's not much else to tell. Mom married Pete and they had Noah. Things went from bad to worse at the house and I had to get a job just to keep the roof over our heads. I started bussing tables at the café up the street." Buddy came to the door and sat to watch and Katherine sighed. "I had a dog once."

"Yeah?"

"Yeah. His name was Monster. Ugliest mutt you ever saw."

"But you loved him."

"I did."

"What happened to him?"

A shudder rippled through her. "When I came home from school one day, he was gone. I was heartbroken. Dad later confessed he'd sold him for ten bucks so he could buy his alcohol." Tears welled and she blinked them back then drew in a deep breath. "Anyway—"

His hand gripped hers and she met his gaze. "I'm sorry," he said.

"I got over it."

"I don't think you did."

A soft, humorless laugh puffed from her. "You don't?"

"When you break down and give Buddy a home, then you'll know you're over it."

For a moment, she didn't answer. Then she nodded to the medicine cabinet above the sink. "There's a suture kit and some numbing meds in there. I can do the stitches if you can get it for me."

He let her change the subject. "Thought you were right-handed."

"I am. Usually. There are some things I've learned to do with whichever hand happens to be free. Sewing is one of those things."

He raised a brow. "Intriguing."

She shrugged. "It came in handy in the field."

Dominic had almost forgotten her days as a tactical medic. He still wanted to hear more of that story. "I'm sure."

He pulled the kit down then threaded the needle for

her—albeit with some difficulty given his rather light-headed state—but he managed.

"You've done that before," she said.

"I went through marshal training with a buddy who was an EMT before he decided he wanted to go into law enforcement. He taught me a few things."

"Like how to thread a needle."

"Yes."

She drew in a deep breath and looked him in the eye. "If I pass out, can you finish it?"

"Are you asking for my help?"

A low laugh escaped her. "Busted."

"Let me do it," he said softly.

She swallowed. "You really can?"

"I can."

"The meds aren't affecting your vision?"

"Not enough to matter." At least he didn't think so.

She returned the needle and thread to him. "Then have at it."

ELEVEN

Thirty minutes later, with Buddy snoozing at her feet and Dominic finally passed out on the couch in the den, Katherine examined her arm in a state of bemusement. It throbbed a painful beat, but Dominic's five stitches were neater than her own would have been.

Letting someone else take charge, take care of her, was a very weird feeling. She wasn't quite sure what to do with it, but thought she wouldn't mind exploring the new emotions—eventually. When Noah was proven innocent and she and Dominic weren't on opposite sides of the fence. So to speak.

But he was right about Monster. She'd never gotten over her father selling him. It had done something to her. Having one more thing that she'd loved ripped from her without any kind of warning had made her more determined than ever not to need anything or anyone. Losing hurt too much. Except Noah. She'd loved him with everything in her.

And she'd eventually lost him, too.

Thinking about her father always unsettled her. She'd give anything to help the man. Mentally, she knew his state of mind and his choices were not necessarily a reflection of his feelings for her, but it still hurt.

It still left a hole only her father's love could fill. Or would letting someone else love her fill it? It was a question she'd never asked herself before. Had never even thought of before. For a while, Noah's presence had helped, but once he was gone, that aching void returned.

What about Dominic? Could he help soothe the pain of her past?

Or was she looking at it all wrong?

She'd never been big on trusting or believing in God, but living with Creed's family had influenced her in so many ways. One of those was teaching her to trust that God had a plan for her life in spite of who her parents had turned out to be. And that if she followed Him, He would never lead her wrong.

Or leave her.

Maybe He was the one who was supposed to fill that emptiness inside her? If she'd let Him.

God, I'm sorry. I've been ignoring You for a while now. I think it's time I turned back to You and let You do some healing in my life. I don't want the past to overshadow my future. I don't want fear to keep me from loving and being loved. Help me—

Her phone rang and she snagged it from the back pocket of her jeans with one hand while she scrubbed away the tears she hadn't realized she was crying with the other.

She didn't recognize the number, but swiped the screen to answer anyway, concerned it could be a patient, her father—or Noah. "Hello?"

"K-Katherine?"

A low gasp slipped from her. She'd hoped he would call, but—"Noah? Are you okay? Where are you?"

"I need you to meet me. Please. I need to see you, to talk to you, but I can't do it over the phone."

"Where?"

"Promise you'll come alone?"

"The marshals and every other alphabet-soup agency are looking for you. You have to turn yourself in."

"I can't!" His hushed shout echoed through the phone line. "I'm at a convenience store, but I have to get out of here before someone recognizes me. Meet me at the old McMillan abandoned barn. You know where I'm talking about."

"Of course, I do."

"Come alone, Kathie, please. Be careful and don't trust anyone because someone's after you, too. I'll tell you more when you get here. I gotta go." Click.

Someone's after you, too.

A chill pebbled her skin and she shuddered. So, she'd been right. She really *had* been the target at the tubing slopes.

But why?

Maybe Noah would have the answer. But she wasn't going alone. *Don't trust anyone.*

But she could trust Creed and the others. And she even trusted Dominic to a certain degree.

She'd take Ben with her.

But then who'd stay to watch after Dominic? Because while Noah had said someone was after her, Dominic was still in danger, as well.

No, she couldn't leave him unprotected. She'd have to take them both with her.

But what if Noah saw them all approach?

He'd run. Then again, Dominic and Ben could hang back and listen in over the phone. Close enough to help if she needed it, far enough away not to spook Noah? It was the ideal plan, but what if Dominic refused to go along with it? After all, he wasn't completely convinced Noah hadn't been the one to kill Carl. He might insist on a whole army of marshals and law enforcement being called in to capture their "dangerous fugitive."

Noah would see it as a betrayal and he'd go back into that vacuum of silence he'd been in for the past three years.

Which wouldn't help anything.

"Ughhh." Her low groan filled the kitchen and Buddy lifted his head then rose to place his snout on her knee, looking up at her with those soft, intelligent brown eyes. "I'm okay, Buddy."

She scratched his ears and pushed her emotions to the side for the moment while she forced her brain to work. Number one, she needed to see Noah and confront him on everything—hear from him about exactly what he was doing and why he was doing it. And that he wasn't a murderer.

Number two, she couldn't leave Dominic alone with a killer after him, but by all appearances, she was in danger, too, so…she needed to figure out how to stay safe while meeting Noah. And finally, number three, she had to get past Ben to get to her garage and into the rental car that had been delivered.

Maybe she should call Regina?

But Regina would have a fit about her meeting Noah and insist on going with her. And if Noah saw Regina, he'd run. So, Katherine had come full circle.

Buddy backed up and shook himself then walked

to the door indicating he was ready to leave or needed to go out. Katherine stood then paused. "Hey, Buddy, come here." The dog obeyed and sat in front of her. "You just gave me an idea. Wanna go for a walk?"

His ears perked up and his tongue lolled out the side of his mouth while his tail thumped his enthusiasm with the idea.

She occasionally took Buddy for a walk through the town, just because she enjoyed it. And Buddy always seemed to, as well. She got the collar from the laundry room and fastened it around his neck. He sat and waited for her to snap on the leash. "Okay, stay here a second. Stay." He stayed.

Katherine returned to the den and found Dominic still out cold. She hesitated then went to the desk in the corner, pulled out a sheet of paper and a pen, and wrote, "Noah called me. I'm going to meet him and try to talk some sense into him. Like turning himself in. I'm not harboring or hiding him—I just want to talk to him." She wrote the directions to the barn and set the note on the coffee table where Dominic would be sure to see it. When she walked back into the kitchen, Buddy was still waiting patiently for her by the door. "Ready, big guy?"

His tail swished across the floor and his bright eyes glinted his eagerness. She snagged the leash and together they walked out the door.

Ben looked up from the chair she'd placed out there from him. Creed had wanted a visible presence on her home and Ben had agreed to brave the chill. He had a small heat lamp at his feet and a laptop on his knees. "You okay?" he asked.

"I'm fine. Buddy needs to take a little break. I'll be back." All truth.

Ben frowned. "You shouldn't be going out by yourself."

"I'll be fine." She paused. "Is Regina at the station?"

"She is."

"Thanks." She studied the deputy's worried eyes and almost blurted out the reason she needed to take a walk. Only the thought of Noah waiting for her and his cryptic message that she was in danger, too, kept her silent. "We're going around back to the grassy area." But she wasn't stupid. She wasn't going to walk into a potentially dangerous situation without a plan.

The problem was, the clock was ticking and her plan was just a glimmer of an idea.

With a prayer on her lips, she walked down the steps and into the small yard. Buddy finished his business and they made a beeline for the garage.

Within a couple of minutes, she was on the road to the outskirts of town with Buddy next to her and her eye on the rearview mirror. Traffic was light and she didn't notice any unfamiliar vehicles. It wouldn't take Ben long to realize she wasn't coming back anytime soon and he'd probably wake up Dominic. And then they'd find the note and come after her. At least that's the way she envisioned it playing out.

For insurance, when she was almost to the barn, she pulled to the side of the road and tapped a text to Regina. Hi Reg, I'm on the way to meet Noah at the old McMillan barn. Can you head this way in case I need you? Just please don't show yourself until I talk to Noah. Please. She hesitated a fraction of a second then tapped Send.

A glance at the dash clock sent a sliver of urgency through her. It had been thirty-five minutes since Noah's call. The old barn was only about ten minutes from her home, so she needed to find Noah fast. And pray no one had been following her. Still, she took a moment to sit and watch three cars go past. She knew all of the drivers.

On impulse, she pulled out and headed back toward town. After two minutes without seeing another vehicle, she did another U-turn and drove to the abandoned McMillan property. The elder McMillans were now in an assisted living home. Their children were grown and had lives far away from Timber Creek. She'd heard rumors the elder McMillans had agreed to the property to be sold after their deaths; however, as long as they were alive, they held out hope that one of the children would want to return and live there. Katherine believed that hope was in vain but supposed stranger things had happened.

Then she had no more time to think or worry about it. Katherine pulled into the drive and wound her way down the rutted dirt road that used to be smooth and graveled. The barn sat at the edge of the property and backed up to several acres of wooded land.

She drove around to the back and tried to ignore the pounding of her heart. Noah had been barely seventeen when she'd last seen him. Part man, part still kid. He'd turned twenty last month and not a day went by that she didn't think about him, that her heart didn't ache with the loss of their relationship. But, he'd made his wishes clear and she'd finally made the gut-wrenching decision to honor them even though she'd sent cards and money to her mother's home on special occasions like his birthday and holidays. But he'd never acknowledged them and she couldn't dwell on it without having a cry-fest.

Taking a deep breath, she climbed out of the car and Buddy hopped out beside her. She stroked his head and he looked up as though asking what was going on. "I know, Buddy. This is a bit out of your comfort zone. I can sympathize, but Noah's in trouble and I need to help him." Buddy simply watched her, waiting for her to lead him. His absolute trust in her caused a lump to form in her throat. Noah used to look at her that way. "Come on, then, let's go find him."

Dominic read the note for the third time before he crumpled it in his fist. "Has she lost her mind?" he asked Ben.

"Naw, she's just used to doing things on her own and doing them her way."

"Even if doing things her way can get her killed?"

"I'm sure that's not her intention."

"Aren't you worried about her?"

"I'm concerned, but I also know how capable she is."

Dominic tossed the wadded note onto the table, barely able to control his anger. "I should arrest her for harboring a fugitive."

Ben raised a brow. "If she was harboring him, she wouldn't have told you where she was going."

"She didn't leave too long ago. How long will it take to catch up with her?"

"About fifteen minutes or so."

"Then let's go."

Ben's phone rang. "Hold up."

"You can't talk and walk?"

The deputy shot him a dark look. "What's up, Regina?" Dominic waited impatiently while Ben listened. "All right. Hang tight. We'll be there shortly."

"What is it?"

"Katherine texted Regina and filled her in. She's

on her way to the barn, but said she was about twenty minutes out. She was up on the mountain handling a domestic violence call. Said she finally was comfortable leaving to head to the McMillan place."

A knock on the door sent Dominic's blood pressure shooting skyward. Ben opened it and Dominic blinked. "Evan?"

"Yeah. You haven't returned my calls, so I visited with Carl's parents for a bit. They told me where you were staying so I decided to come find you."

"Uh…well, it's good to see you, man, but now's not the best time."

"You're working Carl's case?" Evan asked.

"No. At least not officially, but I am searching for our missing witness—which is kind of related to his case…" He waved a hand in dismissal. "It's complicated." He headed for the steps, and Evan followed.

"I'm guessing now's not a good time."

"Right, I'm really sorry."

"Anything I can do?"

Dominic hesitated. "Yeah. Call and check on Leon. He's talking about coming here, too, and while I appreciate the support, I really need to focus on finding Carl's killer." He shot a glance at Ben. "Unofficially, of course."

"Yeah, sure, of course." A pause. "Don't worry about me, Dom—do what you need to do. I'm going to go see Carl's parents one more time and then I'll head home. I'll call Leon on the way."

"I'm sorry, man."

"It's okay, I promise."

"Thanks. I'll catch up with you later." Dominic

slipped into the passenger seat. Evan already had his phone pressed to his ear.

Once Dominic had his seat belt on, he palmed his phone and dialed Beth's number. Then paused. If he called in reinforcements, Noah could run. Regina was on her way and Ben was with him. Between the three of them, surely they would have the element of surprise and could take the kid down with minimal fuss.

And besides, he'd admit the thought of Katherine possibly being caught in the crossfire terrified him.

TWELVE

"Noah?"

She'd been waiting a good three minutes. She glanced at her watch. If he didn't hurry up, there was the risk of Dominic or Regina catching up and scaring Noah off. Assuming he was still here.

"Come on, Noah, where are you?"

Buddy sat beside her, ears pricked, nose wiggling in the wind. He turned his head to look behind them, his fur rising. A low growl slipped from his throat.

She spun, trying to see the threat Buddy had sensed. "I know you're here. Show yourself."

Noah stepped out from behind the old tractor that had been parked next to the barn and left to rust. A momentary pang of sadness hit her that the place was so neglected. She and Noah had always loved visiting the sweet couple and she understood why Noah had run here. She should have thought of it. Looking at her little brother, seeing him for the first time in three years, sent ripples of shock through her. He was tall, but so very skinny. Not anything like the slightly chubby young man he'd been as a teenager.

"Where'd you get the dog?" he asked.

"His name's Buddy. He's adopted me and I like him so I let him hang around."

"Oh." He nodded then blew out a slow breath. "Wow. You came."

She blinked. "Of course, I came."

He shoved his hands in his pockets and shot a nervous glance around. "You're alone?"

"I'm alone at the moment, but I had to let someone know where I was going." She looked at her phone. "We have about twenty minutes or so before someone comes looking for me."

His brown eyes—exactly like hers—flared and he started to back away.

Katherine held out a beseeching hand. "Don't run yet, Noah, please. I could have lied and said no one was coming, but I was up-front with you. We have some time so talk to me. Why do they think you shot that marshal? I can't believe you'd do that, but with your disappearing act, I can't convince them that you didn't."

He paused then raked a hand through his greasy dark hair. She absently wondered when he'd washed it last. "You actually believe I'm innocent?" he asked. He shoved his hands in his front pockets and scuffed the ground with a toe. Just like he used to do as a kid. Her heart ached.

"Yes. And unless you tell me you did it, I'll keep defending you."

Two fat tears rolled down his pale cheeks, then he sniffed and wiped them away. Katherine wanted to shed a few tears of her own, but she held them back. "I didn't kill anyone," he blurted. "What the news is saying is all lies." His chest rose and fell with his agitated words. "I don't even have a gun—or the kind of long-range rifle

needed to make the shot the media is talking about."
He opened his coat and turned in a circle. "Come pat
me down."

"Noah…"

"Do it. Please." Katherine approached him and did
as he'd asked.

"I'm clean," he said when she stepped back.

Katherine wanted to believe him so very much, but
just because he didn't have the weapon on him at the
moment didn't mean he didn't have one hidden somewhere. She hated that thought, but it was the way her
mind worked. She decided to be happy for the fact that
he didn't have a weapon on him for now. He faced her
again. "That marshal who got shot was working with
Pachinko. I guess they had a falling out and Pachinko
sent someone after him, but it wasn't me."

She gasped. "What? Who's Pachinko?"

"I guess I should start at the beginning."

Katherine shot a quick glance at the long drive.
"Let's move into the barn. I don't like being out in the
open like this."

"Yeah. Yeah. Sorry. I should have thought of that."

Once they were inside the barn, Buddy went exploring and Katherine moved to the window that overlooked
the drive. The glass was mostly crusted over with dirt,
but there was one spot she could see through so she'd
be able to tell if anyone was heading their way. She
wasn't worried about the wooded side of the barn, just
the drive. "Tell me what's going on. And hurry."

He chewed on the edge of a thumbnail and paced
the length of the empty barn before stopping in front
of her. "I saw a murder."

She knew that, of course, but another gasp still

slipped from her. He ignored her. "I knew I was in way over my head and that I needed help. I went to the cops who put me in a little room and brought in the DEA and they said if I'd testify, they'd make a couple of outstanding warrants go away and I'd be in protective custody until the trial."

Still no sign of Regina or anyone else. That was good, but she needed him to keep talking. But…outstanding warrants? She'd address that later. "Who was killed?"

He cleared his throat. "I was…ah…working for someone. I didn't find out until later that he was involved in organized crime, but by then, I was in too deep. I just thought I was doing some petty…stuff." He shifted and flushed then shoved his hands into his coat pockets. "I lifted some stuff."

"Like some cars."

"Oh. You know."

"I know."

"Then yeah, I stole some cars. Nothing that hurt anyone but their pocketbooks and nothing that would come with too much jail time if I got caught." He gave a little shrug. "I was stupid and didn't know it until a few months ago."

The fact that his words were tinged with regret allowed a glimmer of hope to flicker to life. Maybe he could turn his life around after all.

"Anyway," he said, "while in custody of the marshals, someone found the hotel where we were staying and tried to grab me when we walked out one night. Dominic O'Ryan managed to get me away from him, but not before the guy took a chunk out of my side with his knife."

Katherine blinked. "Are you all right?" Dominic had neglected to mention that.

"Yeah. Fine. They had a doctor come look at me. I'm healing. But when a second attack happened, I decided I'd be better off on my own. I felt like someone was feeding Pachinko my location and it was only a matter of time before they succeeded in grabbing me—or killing me. Or both."

"Who was feeding them information? I have a feeling you figured it out."

"I sure did—I just didn't expect to find out quite as soon as I did."

"Go on." Another glance out the window. This time she thought she saw the front grill of a car parked off to the side just over the hill. Her pulse pounded. She needed to know the rest of the story and time was running out.

"So, I wanted to leave and hide out on my own," Noah said, "but I needed money. I know where my boss—ex-boss, I guess—stashed some cash and decided I'd borrow it. So, I slipped away from my guard dogs and hitched a ride to the warehouse. When I got there, imagine my surprise when US Marshal Carl Hammond was there, too."

"Doing what?" She frowned, trying to process everything.

"He was telling the boss that I was missing. Carl wasn't working with me that night, so I'm sure when Dominic found me gone, he called Carl." He hesitated. "The only way I can see Carl beating me there is that he didn't have to beat me. He was already there, and I walked in on their conversation." Noah drew in a deep breath. "It didn't take long to realize that Carl and one of Pachinko's goons—the one we called boss—were on real friendly terms. I started to panic. All I wanted to do at that point was get out of there. Only Carl started talking, planning. He said I had a sister, and they'd grab her to use her for leverage and then kill us both when they lured me there."

The blood must have drained from Katherine's head because for a brief moment, she saw stars. "That's why you were coming to Timber Creek, wasn't it?" she whispered. "To warn me."

"Yeah. Only, on my way out, I must have made some kind of noise, though, and they came after me. I wound up stealing a truck and running. Carl must have called in his partner and the others because they caught up with me. I crashed not too far from that ranch, got out and ran." He rubbed his eyes. "I heard the shots, but I…" He shrugged. "I didn't know what was going on, just that if I could get to the McMillan place, I could actually have a chance to think. I was hiding because I knew they'd be looking all over for me. I just didn't know they wanted to pin the murder on me until I saw the news at the convenience store when I finally got the chance to call you."

"What took you so long to call?"

He scoffed. "When I went into protective custody, they took my phone and refused to give me access to it. They still have it. And when I was running, I didn't exactly have time to find a phone." He fell silent for a moment. "I remembered this place and came here. The fact that it looks like it's been abandoned for a while was a plus for me. As soon as I figured things had died down enough, I walked the two miles to the convenience store up the street and used the phone to get you here. To tell you that you're in danger and need to be careful."

Well, that explained a lot. "Who's your ex-boss? The one who wants you dead? This Pachinko guy you keep mentioning?"

"Yeah. His name is Frederick Pachinko. He's a very bad dude, and you want nothing to do with him, trust me. I just figured it out too late to get out easily. Until I saw him shoot a guy in cold blood." A shudder raced through him. "Then I was done. I knew I had to do something, so I went to the cops. I had a picture on my phone of the dead guy and Pachinko, but not of his actually killing the guy, so that's why they needed my testimony."

Katherine glanced at her watch. Depending on when Ben discovered her gone, she probably had no more than two or three minutes before she could expect him to show up. Probably with Dominic. But at least she had a name for the enemy—and why he was after her.

"Come home with me, Noah. Please. Turn yourself back in to protective custody so you'll be safe."

"You're not listening!" His shout echoed through the barn and she blinked.

Buddy padded back over and sat in front of her, eyeing Noah. She placed a hand on his head. "It's okay, boy."

The dog relaxed against her leg, but stayed put, his gaze still on her agitated brother.

"The marshals are in on it," Noah said. "I can't trust them, and neither can you."

"Not all of them are corrupt, Noah."

"I know that, but I have no idea which ones are and

which ones aren't. And until I figure it out, neither one of us is safe."

A chill skated up her spine. Was he right? After all, Dominic and Carl had been best friends. Unless there was another explanation? "Dominic just saved my life. And Creed's. I really think you can trust him."

Regina's cruiser moved slowly toward the barn, and Katherine knew her time was up.

"Saved your—" He raked a hand over his head. "You can tell me about that later. I have to stay in hiding until the real killer is caught," Noah said, "but if they keep focusing on me, they won't look elsewhere." He grabbed her shoulders and turned her to face him. Buddy growled and gave one short bark. Noah stumbled back and Katherine once again reassured the dog.

Noah drew in a shuddering breath and kept his distance, but his gaze intent on hers. "Please, Katherine, tell them to keep looking. Convince them it's not me. Or at least make them wonder if there's the possibility that someone in their inner circle is the killer. And they need to start looking at Carl Hammond's life outside his job."

She believed him. Relief and fear and love mingled together to leave her feeling mostly fear. For him.

He started backing away. "I've got to go. I can't let them catch me."

"Fine." She pulled her phone from her pocket and pressed it into his hand. "Keep this and use it for emergencies only. I'll get a new one and text you my number. At least you'll have a way to call for help if you need it."

He hesitated then pocketed it.

"Keep it off until you get to where you're going. Then turn it on to read my text and get my number. Text me back to let me know that you got it and that you're okay." She gripped his hand. "Promise me."

"I promise." He swallowed. "Thank you."

Her heart broke. He was going to get caught. She'd made sure that he couldn't get away, but she wasn't going to be the one to hold him against his will. She'd been completely honest about everything, including that they were on a time crunch. But if he somehow managed to get away, she wanted him to have a way to communicate. But she had to try one more time. "Please, Noah, turn yourself in. I've been around Dominic for the past couple days and I believe you can trust him."

"No."

"They're going to catch you one way or another and I'm afraid that if you don't let Dominic be the one to take you in, you might wind up dead. Please!"

He hesitated. "You really trust him?"

"I do."

The barn door swung open and Katherine let out a sharp cry, moving quickly to step between Noah and whatever new threat was coming. Buddy barked and Dominic stepped inside. "Time to stop running, Noah."

When Noah bolted toward the back of the barn, Dominic sighed and met Katherine's gaze. "I've already walked the perimeter of the barn. There's no way out. Does he have a weapon?"

She blinked. "No. I asked him and he said no. He even opened his coat and had me pat him down to prove it."

"Come on, Noah," Dominic called. "You know you're trapped, and I really don't feel like chasing you."

Silence.

Dominic looked at her. "Where does he think he's going?"

Katherine's stunned expression had morphed into a frown. "Noah? He's right. Come on, please! You're just going to make things worse."

More silence. Buddy whined and walked a circle around her. She pulled his leash and he settled next to her.

Dominic pressed a hand to his aching head. He really did not feel like dealing with this. But Carl...

"The storm cellar," Katherine said. "No wonder he wasn't worried about you showing up before he could leave."

"What?"

"The storm cellar has an opening to the outside." She hurried in the direction her brother had gone and Dominic raced after her with Buddy pulling up the rear.

"Ben and Regina are here," he said. "They'll stop him as soon as he steps outside."

"They won't see him. It leads to the woods. We're probably already too late."

Dominic followed her into the barn's office and noted the open hole in the floor. "Oh, you've got to be kidding me." He grabbed his phone and punched two—Ben's number on speed dial.

"He's going into the woods. Don't let him get away."

"What? Where?"

"In the woods somewhere on the other side of the barn." Dominic spun, wobbled a moment when the world spun for a split second, then found his balance and grabbed Katherine's hand to pull her along behind him. "Show me where it comes out."

She hurried with him, her breaths coming faster, her

agitation leaping off her skin. Buddy barked and kept looking at her like he was picking up on her emotions and wanted to know what he could do to help. At the door, she took the lead and ran into the woods, the dog bounding after her. "Noah! Please come back!"

"Where'd he go?"

"I have no idea." She led him just inside the edge of the woods to the opening in the ground. The door was flung back, much like the one in the barn office.

Dominic bit off a groan and turned to Katherine. Buddy paced, his head swinging back and forth between them. "There's got to be a place Noah would run to from here," Dominic said. "Someone he trusts."

"No. I don't think so. He didn't go to any of those initially. He won't go there now."

Regina and Ben caught up with them. "I'll see if I can follow him," Ben said. "Even if I don't catch up with him, maybe I can locate where he comes out of the woods." He took off and Regina stepped to the side to call it in.

"We have to cover all the bases." His head throbbed in time with his heart. Light-headed and hurting, he ignored the pain and focused on pulling his phone from his pocket. He called Beth and filled her in. She promised to send backup ASAP. Then raked him over the coals for not calling sooner. "I know, Beth, I'm sorry, but there's more going on here than I can get into right now." Like the fact that Katherine had left him sleeping and sneaked out of her house to meet Noah. He hung up with Beth and turned his focus back on Katherine. "There are some really bad people after Noah, Katherine. I need you to help me find him before they do."

"I know. He told me about them. About Frederick Pachinko."

"What else did he tell you?"

"That he saw the man shoot someone point-blank. That he didn't realize he was in over his head until that point. And that he wanted out. *Wants* out." She bit her lip and narrowed her eyes. "And that he didn't shoot Carl. He said he overheard a conversation that some guy they call the boss and Carl were talking about kidnapping me and using me to get to Noah."

Dominic's hands clenched.

"In fact," she went on, "he said Carl was the one who set up the attacks on him while he was in your custody."

"What! No way. I don't believe it." Fury at Noah's clear deception—and Katherine's blindness to it—ripped through him. It was all he could do to bite his tongue on the torrent of words that he wanted to spew.

But that wouldn't help anything.

"I know you don't," she said, her voice soft, "but I believe you need to at least consider other suspects."

He drew in a deep breath. A calming breath. "That's the point, Katherine. There aren't any other suspects."

"Of course there are!" Her frustration with him flashed in her gaze and for a moment, a brief moment, he wondered if she was right. "You've got tunnel vision when it comes to Noah and Carl."

The moment passed. "And you don't? Could you really see it if Noah was guilty?"

She hesitated, then sighed. "I don't know. Of course, I don't want to believe he could shoot Carl, but he said something interesting. He said it had to be a long-range rifle that was used to kill Carl. Did you have one of those in your car?"

Dominic stilled, then placed his hands on his hips. "In the trunk."

"Is it still there?"

"I haven't heard any differently, so yes, I would assume so."

"Was there one in the truck he stole?"

"No. According to the owner, there were no weapons in the vehicle. And yes, we checked the man out. He came back squeaky clean."

"Did Noah have time to stop and buy one?"

"Of course not," he snapped. He could see where she was going with this line of questioning and she was right. He'd already thought of it himself and couldn't come up with a satisfactory answer. He'd been hoping Noah could shed some light on the question he knew was coming next.

"Then where did he get the weapon to shoot at you and Carl?"

Dominic pressed his palms to his eyes. "I don't know."

THIRTEEN

Regina walked back over to them, tucking her phone into her pocket. Katherine kept her gaze locked on Dominic's, ignoring the deputy. "Please help him," she whispered. He didn't look away, but his eyes narrowed.

Regina cleared her throat and the moment was gone. "That was Creed," she said. "They're keeping him at the hospital overnight and he wanted to know what was going on. I told him what I knew, but he wants to talk to you two ASAP."

Helicopter blades beat the air above, and Katherine knew they were looking for Noah. Soon the dogs would arrive to track him. She could only pray he found some place safe to hole up until she could convince Dominic to at least listen to Noah's side.

Beth approached, her hazel eyes hard when they met Katherine's. "That was a dumb move, Dr. Gilroy."

"I wasn't trying to be dumb," Katherine said, lifting her chin and refusing to be intimidated. "I was trying to get him to turn himself in. Which is why I left a note as to where I was going and what I was doing and specifically said I'm not trying to help him hide—just help him."

"And that's the only reason you're not in cuffs."

"Lay off, Beth," Dominic said. He placed a hand on Katherine's shoulder. "Let's go. My head's killing me."

He escorted her to the rental car and slid into the passenger seat.

"Could I borrow your phone?" she asked.

He handed it to her. "What happened to yours?"

"I'll tell you in a minute." She tapped a message to Isabelle asking her friend if she could borrow her phone and if so, to meet her at the clinic in fifteen minutes. Katherine waited several seconds before she got an affirmative response then deleted the conversation and handed the phone back to Dominic. She put the car in gear to head down the drive.

"Are you going to tell me what happened to your phone?"

"Yes. After we talk."

"About?"

Once they were on the way back toward town and her home, she shot him a sideways glance. "Can we— um—*you*—try to find another suspect in Carl's murder?" She paused. "Because just *what if* Noah's telling the truth? *What if* Carl was involved in something he shouldn't have been? What if he fell out of favor with whoever he was working with and they killed him and framed Noah?"

"He wasn't involved."

"How do you know? How can you be one hundred percent certain that he wouldn't be involved?"

"The same way you're certain Noah wouldn't be."

Katherine sighed. "I'm not a hundred percent," she said, her voice soft, "but I do want to give him the benefit of the doubt and have someone like you listen to him. Someone in a position to actually investigate his story and prove it one way or another." He stared out the window, but she thought he was thinking.

He finally turned. "Why would Carl do it? Risk everything? His career, his friends, his life? Why?"

"Only Carl can answer that." She paused. "In all the years that you've known him, he never gave you any indication that he might be involved in something shady?"

"No."

Katherine fell silent. There wasn't anything she was going to be able to say that would convince him otherwise. But she had to keep trying. She needed to help Noah and the only person who could really do that was the one who thought he'd killed his partner. "Dominic, I need you to help him. Please. If not for him, then for me." He didn't answer. "I know just saying it can't make you believe it, but I'm not like that person who convinced your father her husband was innocent. I'm just asking you to give Noah the benefit of the doubt. Consider the possibility that he's telling the truth."

He sighed, the sound so weary, her heart quivered. Oh, how she liked this man and wished the circumstances of their meeting were different. "If he's telling the truth," Dominic finally said, "then that means my partner, a man I loved like a brother, who saved my life *several* times, is guilty of…things that…and I can't…even…"

Her fingers curled tight around the steering wheel and she forced calm into her voice. "And Noah *is* my brother. And I know he's not perfect. He admitted he'd done some illegal things and I think he should have to answer for those—at least pay restitution or do community service—but you said yourself, you never thought he was violent. Well, he's not. He didn't kill Carl and I need your help to prove it." She paused. "And if you can't do that, then I'm not sure where we can go from here."

He fell silent and so did she, her heart aching, mind whirling.

"Okay," he said after several minutes.

Katherine pulled into the parking space at the clinic and Buddy popped his head over her seat to rest his nose on her shoulder. She scratched his jaw and turned her attention to her passenger. "Okay, what?"

"Okay. I'll consider other options. Maybe Noah got it wrong and only thought he saw Carl there with whoever their boss was. Maybe there's another explanation." He paused. "You're right. I keep coming back to the fact that I never saw Noah act violent in any way. Not that there's not a first time for everything, but…"

"He was always the one who wanted to take in the stray animals, help the homeless on the street, be the first to pitch in to help a friend. At least the Noah I knew. I'm not saying people don't change and I know it's been three years, but, unless he's become an Oscar-worthy actor, that guy back in the barn isn't a killer. He's a scared kid in over his head and needs someone to fight for him."

He nodded. "You know, I said Carl never gave me any indication that he might be involved in something illegal, but…I might be wrong."

"What do you mean?"

"Your questioning just brought some things to mind. Incidents that he explained away."

"Like?"

"We had one other witness who was going to testify against Pachinko. He committed suicide while on our watch." He rubbed his eyes. "The ME ruled it suicide anyway."

"But you don't think it was?"

"I never saw it coming. The guy was talking about the future and starting over. We were at a hotel and I left to pick up food in the lobby. When I came back to the room, the bedroom door was shut and the shower was on. Carl said the guy would be out in a few minutes. We ate and when the shower kept running and the witness never appeared, I went looking for him. He was in the tub, his wrists slashed."

Katherine sucked in a sharp breath. "Oh, no."

"I've always wondered where he got the razor."

"Carl gave it to him?"

He shrugged. "Carl said there was a bag of toiletries in the bathroom and he went through them and must have missed the razor." He sighed. "He was depressed for months after that, but…" Dominic rubbed his eyes. "When we find him, I promise I'll listen first—and make sure he gets to tell his story."

Relief brought a sudden rush of tears to her eyes and she had to blink to clear her vision. "Thank you."

Regina pulled in next to Katherine along with two US marshals, one of whom was driving another vehicle. Katherine raised a brow. "Protection? Or do they think I'll lead them to Noah?"

"Probably a little bit of both."

At least he was honest.

"That's my car," he said. "The one Carl and I were driving when we were chasing your brother. Guess they figure I can start driving again." His gaze lingered on it and the marshal who stepped out of the driver's seat. Owen, Beth's partner. Dominic rolled his window down. Owen walked over and dropped the keys into Dominic's outstretched hand. Dominic stared at the keys. "Carl drove most of the time."

"I still can't believe he's gone."

"I know." Owen clapped Dominic on his shoulder and headed toward Beth who climbed out of her own vehicle.

"He and Carl were good friends?"

"They'd known each other since elementary school and while they weren't best friends, yeah, they were pretty close."

Dominic reached for the door.

"I need to tell you something," Katherine said.

He paused then tilted his head and eyed her warily. "Okay."

"I think I can find Noah, but you have to strengthen your promise talk to him before you call in reinforcements."

"Katherine—"

"I know. I know."

He fell silent. "It would mean slipping away from our guard dogs." A pause. "I could get in huge trouble for that. Not to mention that it could be very dangerous for both of us."

She winced. But for Noah… "I know. And I wouldn't ask if I didn't feel like having you talk to him—mostly listen to him—would allow him to believe someone is on his side. And he would come in on his own if he felt like he could trust you. I'd ask Creed to go with us, but…"

"It would go better for Noah if he quit running."

"That goes without saying, but as long as he feels like turning himself in is a waste of time because no one is

going to listen to him, then he's just going to keep running and hiding." She pressed cool fingers against her
burning eyes. She would not cry.

"And if he doesn't come peacefully?"

Katherine swallowed. "Then you can do what you
need to do—short of...you know...shooting him."

"If he has a weapon—"

"He doesn't."

"That you know of. I can't take your word for that.
You've worked alongside law enforcement. You know
how this works." She did, but stayed silent, giving him
time to think. He sat quiet and thoughtful. Finally, he
nodded. "I said I'd listen and I will."

More relief flooded through her. "He's going to be
mad at first so you'll have to stay out of sight until I can
convince him that you're there to help."

Dominic nodded again. Beth approached and he
rolled down his window. "Everything all right in here?"

"We're fine, Beth." Dominic climbed out.

"Katherine?"

She turned to see Isabelle being detained by the two
marshals. "Let her through, please."

They did and Isabelle hurried over to Katherine and
threw her arms around her. "I'm so glad you're okay."

"Thank you." Katherine felt a slight tug on her back
jeans pocket and knew Isabelle had slipped her phone
into it. Gratitude for this friend shot through her. She
gave Isabelle a tight squeeze then stepped back.

"You're sure you're okay?" Isabelle asked.

"For now." She introduced her to Dominic and the
others.

"Mac's back in town and said to tell you to let him
know if there's anything he can do to help."

"If he's working tomorrow, I'm sure Creed will put him on guard duty."

"He's off for the next couple of days, but said he'd volunteer his time if you needed him."

"I think we'll be all right. Let Creed make that call."

"Sure."

"Come on," Beth said. "We don't need to be standing out here like this."

Isabelle backed away with a wave. "I'll talk to you tomorrow."

"Thanks. I appreciate it."

Once they were inside, Regina looked at Dominic. "How's the head?" she asked.

"Surprisingly, a little better." He dropped into the kitchen chair and Buddy walked over to rest his snout on Dominic's knee.

"I think you've made a friend," Katherine said.

Dominic smiled and scratched the dog's ears. Buddy closed his eyes, his blissful expression bringing a laugh from Katherine. Her heart flipped, then finally settled to pound out a rapid beat. She looked away from the handsome pair. She'd come to care for these two males much more than she wanted to admit.

Dominic stood and checked his phone. "Excuse me a minute—I need to make a call." He slipped down the hall toward her bedroom and Katherine figured he wanted some privacy. From her or Regina, she wasn't sure. Maybe both. She could only pray he wasn't calling about Noah.

Uncertainty nearly made her sick. Had it been a mistake to trust him? Would she be setting Noah up to be killed by bringing Dominic along with her?

Katherine offered Buddy a bowl of water, then paced the kitchen while Regina stood in the living area tapping her phone screen. When she finished, she walked over to Katherine. "I'm going to have a look around the perimeter then let Ben take over guard duty while I run home and check on my mother. He should be here in about five minutes."

"How's she doing?"

"She's okay. The fall didn't do much damage, thankfully, but I think we're getting to the point that we're going to have to find a place for her. For her own safety." Regina's eyes clouded and Katherine's heart ached for her friend.

"I'm sorry."

"I am, too." She sighed and shook her head. "Anyway, one of the marshals left and the other is watching the place. You should be fine until Ben gets here."

"All right." Having Regina gone would make it easier to slip away from the place undetected. Guilt speared her, but she had to do this for Noah. "Thank you, Regina."

"Of course. Be safe." Regina left and Katherine listened. The faint sound of Dominic still talking reached her and she pulled out the phone Isabelle had slipped into her pocket when she'd hugged her. She tapped a text to Noah as promised, giving him the new number and asking if he was okay, and prepared herself to wait for him to answer.

But she didn't have to.

For now, came his instant response. I have a place where I think I'll be safe. I'm walking in now.

Quickly, she traced his location using the app that would allow her to find her phone. Then texted Where? Just because she wanted to hear from him again.

No answer.

Noah?

I'm fine now. Please don't trust anyone. Especially the people who were working with Carl. I don't know that Dominic is dirty, but I don't know that he isn't, either.

I'm working on it. I really don't think Dominic's involved.

Are you willing to stake my life on it?

Chills danced up her arms. Was she?

Dominic walked back into the kitchen. "Everything okay?" she asked. *Please don't betray me. Please don't make me regret asking you for help.*

"Yes, I think so. As okay as it can be." He swiveled his gaze to the den then back to her. "Are we alone?"

"For about five minutes, I think."

"Good. If we go down through the clinic, can we get out of it without anyone seeing us?"

"There's the emergency exit, but the alarm will sound."

"That won't work."

She drew in a breath, studied him. Could she trust him? The question screamed through her mind. But did she have a choice? Her gut said she could.

"Katherine?"

Trust him. She really had to. "Okay, I've been thinking about this and may know another way. Follow me."

Dominic fell into step behind her. She led him into the clinic which bustled with activity. "What are we doing?"

"Looking for someone."

"Who?"

"Katherine?" A man's voice stopped them. Dominic turned to see an older gentleman in his early seventies approaching. Katherine looked at Dominic. "Him."

Dr. N. Barry, M.D. was stitched on the left side of the man's white lab coat. "I didn't think you were working today."

"I'm not here officially. I just came to see you. Ned, this is Dominic. He's one of the marshals looking for Noah. Could we talk for a moment?"

Dominic noticed the doctor didn't ask what was going on with Noah or why the marshals were looking for him. The news was all over the town—and beyond.

"Of course." Ned led them down the short hallway to an office.

Once inside the door, Katherine said, "Could we borrow your car?"

He blinked. "What?"

"Just for a couple of hours. It's important."

"Does this have anything to do with the fact that someone shot up your vehicle?"

"Yes."

They could use the rental, but they both knew a tracker could be on it. Or someone would spot her leaving in it. The rental car had to stay where it was parked.

Ned studied her for a moment, his sharp brown eyes assessing. He turned his gaze Dominic. "I need her back in one piece. I don't have time to go doctor shopping."

The concern beneath the words was clear. "I understand, sir. That's the plan. To return all *three* of us—and your vehicle—in one piece."

The man nodded, walked to his desk and opened a drawer. He tossed the keys to Katherine who snagged them midair. "Thank you, Ned."

"Be careful. And don't you dare tell Sophie that I let you do this."

"Not a word, I promise."

Katherine led Dominic to the back of the building to a door off to the side and peered out.

"See anyone?" he asked.

"No. We're in the clear. Come on. This is the staff parking area. I park in the garage because I live here, but Ned's car is there." She pointed at the sporty little red Mercedes.

Dominic let out a short laugh. "Seriously?"

"It was a birthday present from his wife two years ago."

"Nice wife. The Sophie he mentioned?"

"That's the one."

He climbed into the passenger seat and ran a hand over the leather. "Wow."

"So, you wouldn't be upset if your wife went out and bought you one without telling you?"

"Not even a little bit." He paused. "Would you buy your husband a gift like this?"

"Only if I knew we could afford it and he wouldn't be upset." Their eyes met for a fraction of a second before she cleared her throat and let out a low laugh, cranked the engine and pulled out of the parking lot.

His heart hammered because with each passing moment, he found himself more and more drawn to this special woman. What scared him was he also found himself selfishly wanting to believe she was right about Noah—for all their sakes. Because if Noah was guilty, he had a feeling he would have to kiss his chance at a shot with Katherine goodbye before he'd ever get a chance to know what it was like to kiss *her*.

He pushed his feelings aside and cleared his throat. "Thank you for trusting me."

She flicked him a glance. "I'll confess to having second thoughts when you disappeared into the back of the house to have your phone call."

Was she wanting to know who he was talking to? A pang of discomfort slid through him. Should he tell her that he'd been clearing this whole thing with his director? She was trusting him. Didn't he owe her the same? No, he didn't, but he wanted to be straight with her.

"I had to call my director, Katherine."

"What!" She shot him a quick glance before turning back to the road. Her fingers clamped the wheel. "How could you?" she whispered.

"I didn't tell him where we were going, just that we had a good idea how to find Noah and had a plan to get him to turn himself in. He wanted to argue about it, but he finally agreed to let me do this."

"So, you're really going to keep your promise?"

"I am."

"Okay, then."

She fell silent and he cleared his throat. "Where are we going?"

"A little place between here and Asheville. It's just a fifteen-minute drive, but in season, it's quite a little tourist hotspot because of the views of the mountains and the time-shares going up. Right now, it's starting to calm down as no one except the locals are real excited about riding out the winter months up here. But there's a small hostel that's pretty popular because it's cheap, but clean and has good food." She handed him the phone. "Can you plug this in for me?" He did, and the map came up on the screen. She pointed. "There. I gave Noah my phone right before you showed up. Isabelle slipped me hers when she hugged me. I texted Noah a little while ago and he said he'd arrived at the location he was aiming for. I tracked him real fast and know exactly where he is. I don't how he got there without someone recognizing him from his picture on the news, but he's there."

Dominic ran a hand over his face. "What if someone tries to use your phone to track you?"

She stilled then shot him a narrow-eyed look. "I thought about that and told Noah to turn it off once we'd communicated. I tracked him really fast. I know someone else could do the same if they were watching and waiting for my phone to come online, but I was hoping it was worth the risk." She paused. "Now you've got me worried."

"If he turned it off immediately, there's a good chance he's in the clear, but…"

"Yeah. If he didn't—" She bit her lip and blinked. "I just wanted to be able to find him before Pachinko's goons do," she said, her voice low.

"I know." He glanced at the ETA on the screen. "We're three minutes away from him. Why don't you call him and see if he's turned it off?"

Katherine voice activated the call and they listened to it ring. Once. Twice. Three times. The fourth ring went to her voice mail and she ended the call with a frown. "He didn't turn it off, but he's not answering, either. He'd have that phone right at his fingertips. He has this number so he knows it's me. I have a bad feeling about this." She spun the wheel into the parking lot of a hostel and Dominic's nerves twitched. She parked. "I can't believe he wound up here."

"Why not?"

"Because my dad stays here occasionally. When he

manages to scrounge up enough money for a night or two—or when he'll let me pay for it."

Dominic eyed the dark sedan parked in front of the door.

With the engine running. "That doesn't look right."

"I see it."

"There's a driver, too."

"Like he's waiting for someone to come out. You were right," she said, her voice soft. "They tracked the phone."

"Thinking they were tracking you. I'm going to have to call this in, Katherine."

"I know."

He grabbed his phone and dialed. When Beth answered he gave her the short version of where they were. "I'll text you the location. We're going to need some backup."

He hung up on the beginning of her tirade, not blaming her for being furious. If the situation was reversed, he'd feel the same way.

"I led them right to him, didn't I?" Katherine asked. She shoved open her door to climb out.

"You didn't. Noah didn't follow your instructions to turn it off. What are you doing?"

"Getting to Noah before they do." Before she could dart for the door, it opened and a dark-haired, dark-eyed man emerged with Noah in tow. A weapon glinted in the sunlight. Dominic pulled his gun, stepped out of the car and aimed at the man holding Noah. "Stop! Federal agent!"

FOURTEEN

Katherine froze, her gaze meeting Noah's. His frantic eyes darted between her and Dominic then back to her. The man behind him shoved Noah toward the car and Katherine's heart pounded in a frantic beat. "Let him go!"

The gun swung in her direction and she ducked behind her open door, expecting to hear the crack of the weapon, but it didn't come.

"Drop it!" Dominic mirrored her position behind the passenger door. He glanced at her for a millisecond. "I don't have a shot."

Noah acted. His elbow went back, and he spun to kick his attacker in the knee then took off toward Katherine. The man let out a harsh scream, dropped behind the vehicle and fired at Noah's fleeing back.

Noah went down.

"Noah!" Katherine wanted more than anything to bolt to her brother, but held back to see the man jump into the sedan. Tires squealed and peeled away from the hostel. Katherine ran to Noah's side.

She dropped to her knees next to him. "Noah?"

He started to roll to his back, and she stopped him. "Stay still. Just be still for a minute."

"I'm sorry, Katherine, I didn't turn the phone off like you told me to."

"I kind of figured that out, but don't worry about that right now. I'm just glad you're alive." She pressed her hands against the wound, grateful it wasn't bleeding much, but aware that could change, depending on where the bullet lodged. She needed supplies.

Dominic stepped up beside her and placed a hand on her shoulder. "Ambulance is on the way. Ten minutes out."

"Good. In the meantime, I need to make sure he's going to be all right. Can you see if there's a first-aid kit or something in the hostel?"

"Sure." He headed for the door and Katherine glanced at the onlookers.

"Anyone else hurt?" she asked.

The man closest to her met her gaze and shook his head. "No."

"The guy terrorized us, but he didn't hurt anyone," another said.

She glanced at Noah's face. He was staring at her with a coldness that shot her anxiety levels through the roof. "You lied to me. I trusted you and you lied."

"I had to bring him, Noah. And I didn't lie about anything. Dominic wants to help you. He gave his word he'd listen to your side of the story. I promise." She paused. "If I'm wrong, I'll make it right and get you somewhere safe."

His glare lessened only a fraction. "You won't do anything against the law. You and I both know that."

He was right. She wouldn't. "But I can hire the best attorney in the state of North Carolina."

Dominic returned and handed her a first-aid kit.

With precise movements, she did what she could with what little she had to treat the wound. It wasn't perfect, but it would do until she could get Noah to the hospital.

Sirens sounded in the distance and drew closer with each passing second. "Did you get a license plate on that car?" she asked Dominic.

"A partial. I've already passed it on." He turned to Noah. "I'm sorry, kid, but I've got to cuff you."

Without taking his eyes from hers, Noah simply held out his nonwounded arm and Dominic wrapped the cuff around his wrist. "Do you know who tried to grab you?"

Noah winced at the pressure she was putting on his wound, but ground his teeth and said, "I don't know his name, but I recognized him even with the ski mask on. He's one of Pachinko's puppets. Low on the food chain. And since he failed to get me, he'll probably be floating in a lake somewhere before the end of the day."

"We'll let you look at some mug shots of known organized crime members. Maybe one of them will be your guy."

"Yeah, I'll look."

Katherine shuddered at the thought of the people Noah had gotten involved with but was thankful that was coming to an end. Hopefully with him alive and living nearby so she could help him—and keep an eye on him. Assuming they could find a way to keep him out of prison. *Please, God, give Noah a second chance with me.*

The ambulance arrived along with other law enforcement vehicles and personnel including Beth Wilson, Owen Charles and two more US marshals. Beth approached and Dominic stood. "Hang tight while I handle this."

"We'll be putting Noah into the ambulance," Katherine said. "I assume you'll be going to the hospital with him?"

"Someone will. Probably Beth. I'll follow and the others will be there, too. We can at least make sure he arrives there safely."

"Thank you."

Beth stopped in front of Dominic. "I see you went rogue again, O'Ryan. Gonna have to let the director know about this."

"Sorry to burst your bubble, but the director already knows and I had his blessing." He took a smidgeon of pleasure at the surprised look on her face, but refused to gloat. "In the meantime, since this isn't my case and all, I assume you won't let me ride with them in the ambulance."

"Give the man a gold star."

"Back off, Beth," Owen said.

"No, you back off. This has to be done by the book or Pachinko is going to walk."

Dominic held up his hands in surrender and she turned her scowl on her partner. "I'll be riding with him. See you at the hospital." She turned her attention to those loading Noah into the back of the ambulance.

Owen looked at Dominic. "Sorry. She's had a bee in her bonnet ever since Carl was killed."

"It's all right. She's grieving like the rest of us. I'll just follow behind." Katherine caught Dominic's eye and nodded.

"See you there," he said.

"Thank you." She climbed into the back of the ambulance with Beth on her heels. The paramedic who'd gotten Noah started on oxygen and an IV looked up at her. "You've got medical training?"

"I'm a doctor."

"Cool. Welcome aboard. I'll follow your lead. My name's John."

"Thanks, John." Katherine turned to her brother, who was still conscious, but in obvious pain. "Noah, are you allergic to anything new?"

"No."

She looked at John. "Morphine. Eight milligrams."

"Coming right up."

And so it went with the paramedic assisting her in monitoring Noah until they arrived at the hospital. Beth was quiet, but she didn't miss a thing.

Twenty minutes later, Noah was in a room while they waited for the surgeon to get to the hospital. Beth had cuffed him to the bed and Katherine didn't bother to protest, knowing it would fall on deaf ears. Noah wasn't going anywhere except to surgery. Fortunately, he had enough pain meds in him that he was comfortable, if a little loopy. Owen stood by the door watchful and quiet.

Dominic entered the room and Noah bristled. Katherine placed a hand on his. "Give him a chance, Noah."

He pursed his lips then gave a slow nod, his eyes tracking Dominic. "You'll really listen?"

"Yeah. I'll listen."

Beth scoffed and Katherine shot her a scowl. Thankfully the woman kept any words she might have wanted to utter to herself.

Dominic leaned a shoulder against the wall and crossed his arms. "Katherine's explained a few things to me, but can you go over everything that led you to believe Carl was involved Pachinko?"

Owen sucked in a quick breath, and Katherine thought his face paled.

"What?" Beth straightened. "You can't be serious."

"I'm giving him a chance to explain," Dominic said. "If you can't listen without interruption, will you kindly leave?"

"This is my case."

"*Our* case," Owen said, his voice soft.

Beth sighed. "Whatever. Either way, I'm not the one who'll be leaving."

Owen shot her a scowl. "Give him fifteen minutes to hear the kid out. I want to hear it, too."

She rolled her eyes, but said, "Fine."

Dominic turned back to Noah and nodded. "Again, why do you say Carl was involved with Pachinko?"

"Because, after I left the safe house—which I was still skeptical about being all that safe—I went to the warehouse where Pachinko keeps a stash of cash. I was planning to...um...borrow some just until the trial." His eyes clouded. "Because I was still planning to show up for the trial, but I figured I had a better chance of surviving until then if I was on my own."

Another scoff from Beth had Katherine gritting her teeth. Noah either didn't hear her or chose to ignore her. "Anyway, at the warehouse, I overheard several people talking and making plans to grab Katherine in order to get to me. Pachinko wasn't there, of course, he was still in prison, but the people who work for him are loyal." He drew in a shuddering breath. "I had to warn her, but you took my phone and I didn't know who to trust. Which is why I ran here." His words were sluggish and slightly slurred and Katherine could only pray he'd manage to stay awake long enough to tell the rest of his story.

"You heard them," Dominic said. "Could you be mistaken about that?"

"No, because I saw them, too. And after having Carl as one of my bodyguards for the past several weeks, I have no doubt about who I was seeing and hearing. He was involved with Pachinko. And there were a couple of other people there, too. The four of them were buddy-buddy."

"Four?" Katherine asked. "You didn't say anything about another person."

Her brother shrugged and his eyes drifted shut.

Katherine squeezed his hand. "Noah?"

He let out a low groan and she waited patiently for him to win the battle of forcing his eyes back open. "What? Sorry. Um…"

"The men who were there? Who were they?"

"I didn't know who two of them were. Still don't. One was kind of in the shadows and didn't say much. Same with the other. But they were all tight. Like they'd been working together for a while. Only, I'd never heard one of their voices before that night. It sounded kind of familiar, but I couldn't place it." He frowned. "I think I should know who it is, but I can't…" His eyes started to shut once more.

"Other marshals?" Dominic asked.

"Oh, please." Beth's words exploded from her lips. "Are you really buying this?"

Katherine was grateful when Dominic ignored the woman and kept his eyes locked on Noah.

"I have no idea," Noah said. The room fell silent and Noah squirmed, and Katherine could tell he was losing the battle against the drugs that wanted to drag him under. "Do you believe me?" he mumbled.

Dominic sighed and rubbed his forehead. "I don't know what to believe, but I…can't deny I can hear the ring of truth in your words."

"Well…thank you. I think."

Even Beth had gone silent although her glare could still cut through steel. Owen didn't seem happy with Noah's revelations, either, but who could blame them? Of course they didn't want to believe some of their own could be involved with an organized crime boss. Katherine cleared her throat. "Could I have a few minutes alone with Noah, please?"

"No," Beth said, "sorry."

Katherine scowled. "Then at least pretend not to listen." She turned back to Noah. "Why did you refuse to talk to me after I said you could come live with me?"

"What are you talking about? Mom said you called her and told her that I wanted to live with you."

"Exactly, I did."

"But," he continued as though she hadn't spoken, "that you didn't want to hurt my feelings by saying no and needed her to break it to me gently." Katherine gasped, his words a punch to her gut. His eyes widened at her reaction. "Kat?" He sounded uncertain, the frown deepening the lines between his brows.

"Noah," she said when she finally found her voice, "I didn't… I never… That's not…"

"She lied." His flat words nearly broke her heart.

"Yeah," Katherine whispered, "she did."

Noah's eyes reddened and, just like in the barn, two tears rolled down his cheeks.

"I'm sorry, Noah, but I begged her to let you come live with me. I wanted you so very much."

"I can't believe her. I think I hate her." He dropped his head back against the pillow, his eyes closing.

Katherine leaned in. "No, Noah, please don't hate her. The hate will only destroy you from the inside. Just let it go and realize that we have a new start. Whatever you need, I'm here for you."

"Thank you," he whispered. His hand tightened around hers and he mumbled something she didn't catch.

"What?"

His lids lifted. "Why does she hate me so much?"

"She doesn't, Noah. Not at all. It's…it's not you."

"Okay, then why does she hate you so much?"

Katherine swallowed and looked down. "Why do you ask that?"

"Because once I got past the age of needing a baby-sitter, she did everything in her power to turn me against you. I never could figure it out and she wouldn't tell me why."

Katherine pressed her fingers to her burning eyes. "Because I chose my father over her and she's never been able to forgive me for it."

"Oh." His gaze met hers. "Why did you choose him?"

"For a lot of reasons. Mostly because he needed me. I was afraid he'd die if I left with her."

"I can understand that. You're a good person, Katherine. Can you forgive me for not speaking to you? For refusing your calls?"

"Of course." The drugs had kicked in big time, and he was just about out of fight. She reached for his hand, entwining her fingers around his. Anger with her mother nearly burned a hole in her heart, but she refused to let it spoil this moment. "I love you, Noah."

"I love you, too." His eyes closed and while more tears slid down his temples, his features lost that hard, pinched look and he reminded her of the little boy she used to know.

Now they just had to find the killer who was responsible for trying to frame him for murder.

Dominic had to admit being touched by the siblings' reconciliation. He was glad they'd discovered the truth and managed to put the past behind them before the door opened and Noah was wheeled off to surgery. Beth had followed the gurney, but shot him a look he interpreted to mean, "Don't do anything stupid."

He ignored her and placed his hands on Katherine's shoulders. "He'll be well guarded, don't worry."

"But I do worry. Will this change anything? Like will they still let him avoid jail time for his testimony?"

"Yes. He's a small fish. They want the big guys at the top and they can't get them without Noah."

"Good. That's good."

"But he needs to behave himself from now on."

"I don't think he'll have a choice." She bit her lip. "Does this mean you believe him? That he didn't kill Carl?"

He sighed. "It means I'm okay with giving him the benefit of the doubt at the moment." Tears filled her eyes and Dominic couldn't stand it anymore. He gave a gentle tug and she fell against him, shoulders shaking as she silently cried. Her quiet sobbing was almost more heartbreaking than if she'd wailed and pounded on his chest.

So, he stood there and let her cry, rubbing her back and wishing he could take her pain away. And then it was over almost as fast as it had started. She stepped back, swiped her eyes and sighed. "Sorry. I didn't mean to break down on you."

"It's perfectly fine. Understandable even. Everyone needs a good cry every so often and I'd say you have more reason than most."

"You must have sisters."

"I have two. Why?"

"Because you didn't run when the tears started. You knew exactly what to do." She gave a breathless little laugh that held very little humor. "They trained you well."

He smiled. He couldn't help it. His gaze dropped to her lips and she stilled. Then shifted, a subtle invitation that said she wasn't opposed to him closing the distance between them and kissing her.

So…he did.

Her arms slid around his waist and she kissed him back. It was tender and new. Sweet and searching, with a hint of passion held in check. When he lifted his head and saw the question in her eyes, reason intruded. Her brother was still an unresolved issue. He was going to have to deal with that before he could even think about pursuing anything of a romantic nature with her. But he couldn't simply kiss her then push her away—or apologize for kissing her. Mostly because he wasn't sorry.

But…

He closed his eyes. "I like you a lot, Katherine."

"I like you a lot, too, Dominic."

"But I can't…we can't… I mean, it's not that I don't want to see if there's…"

"I know."

"It's just that I don't know what's going to happen with your brother and I have to stay professional—" And boy, did he just mess that up big time. He sighed. "I'm not expressing myself very well right now."

"It's okay, Dominic, truly."

"Because," he went on, wanting to make sure it really was okay, "what if your brother isn't quite as innocent about Carl's death as his protests want us to believe? Like maybe, he didn't actually pull the trigger, but…"

She sighed and lowered her chin. "I don't think you'll discover that's the case, but I can understand your dilemma. Please, don't worry about it." They fell silent and Dominic struggled for the right words and stayed quiet when he couldn't find them. "I think I'm going to go visit Creed while Noah's in surgery," she finally said.

"Do you mind if I come with you?"

"Of course not." They stepped out of the room and found Ben and Regina in the hallway. "We're going to see Creed," she told them.

Regina looked up from her phone. "We'll go with you."

"How's your mother?" Katherine asked.

The deputy shrugged. "About the same."

Dominic wondered what was going on with the woman's mother, but didn't figure it was his place to ask. Regina looked at him. "She has dementia."

"Oh. I'm sorry." He grimaced. "And I'm sorry if it's lame to say I'm sorry."

The woman smiled. "It's not lame. Thank you."

When they reached Creed's room, they found him sitting up in bed and on the phone. He motioned them in. "I'll call you back later. Thanks." He hung up and raised a brow. "What's going on?"

"Noah's in surgery," Katherine said. "We wanted to make sure you were still breathing."

The man grunted and pressed a hand to his head. "I am, thanks to you two." He scowled at Katherine. "That was a dumb thing you did."

"You're welcome."

He shot her a half smile. "You okay?"

"I'm not sure *okay* is the word, but I'm hanging in there."

Creed nodded then looked at Dominic. "You got an update for me?"

"Nothing your deputies haven't already told you. Basically that Noah's in surgery to remove the bullet, but looks like he'll be fine." He drew in a deep breath. "He gave us some information that we're going to look into. Honestly, I'm not sure I expect anything to come from it, but I promised to check it out, so I'll do so."

Creed nodded. "Good. Keep me in the loop?"

"Of course."

"Good. Now I think I know how your head feels and you have my sympathies."

"Which is our cue to leave," Katherine said.

Dominic took her hand. "Get some rest," he told Creed. "We'll come back later."

The sheriff's eyes were already closing as they headed for the door. "Waiting room?" Dominic asked.

"Yes, please."

Once they were settled in the chairs with Ben and Regina in the hallway, Dominic caught her studying him. "What?"

"Tell me about your family."

He shrugged. "Not a whole lot to tell. Mom's a schoolteacher. She's taught fifth grade ever since I can remember. Dad's on disability but does a lot of wood-working to keep from being bored. He sells his stuff to people all over the country."

"Sounds like a talented man."

"Very. I think you'd like them."

"Well, if they're anything like you, then I'm sure I would."

His heart warmed and he had to steel himself against taking her hand and pulling her close. He cleared his throat. "Like I said, I have two sisters. One's married and has two boys—twins who just turned three."

"Oh, wow. I bet they're fun."

"They're a blast. The other sister, Carla, is working on her PhD in pharmacology. Not married and doesn't seem to be in any hurry to change that."

"Good for them." She frowned. "So, how's your father doing these days? You said he was on disability."

He shrugged. "It's been seven years since the shooting. He has his good days and bad, but at least he can walk and do most of the things he wants to do. He's learned to enjoy life again. It's not the same, of course, but even different can be good."

She nodded. "You're close to them all."

"Very. I don't get to see them nearly as much as I'd like to, but yeah, we're close. We FaceTime or talk at least once a week."

A wistful expression, so fleeting he would have missed it had he blinked, crossed her face, then she simply drew in a breath and leaned her head back against the chair. "I need to go find my father when this is all over. Check on him. I would have gone on one of my days off if things hadn't gone haywire."

"You mean if you hadn't had to rescue me, huh?"

She smiled. "Yes."

"I heard you say your mother was angry with you for choosing your dad over her but missed the rest of the conversation as I was really trying not to eavesdrop. Why'd you choose your father over your mother?"

For a moment, she didn't answer, didn't open her eyes, didn't move. Then slid him a sideways glance and seemed to make up her mind about something. "It wasn't like I thought I would be getting the better end of the deal or anything. My parents had been fighting for as long as I could remember. But, the night before Mom left, I overheard an argument where she threw it in his face that she hadn't wanted me in the first place. That I was the reason she was so miserable."

Dominic's heart thudded. "Wow. That's...that's..."

"Harsh?"

"And beyond."

"My parents weren't married when Mom got pregnant. She was only seventeen and Dad was eighteen. Dad told me later—after I demanded an explanation—that her parents, my grandparents, were furious with her for ruining her future." She wiggled her fingers around the last three words. "They didn't want me, either. They wanted her to put me up for adoption."

"Why didn't she?"

"Because Dad said he wanted me." He frowned and she sighed. "I know his actions don't match up with the words, but that's what he said." She paused. "Truly, I think it was my mom he wanted and as long as I was around to tie them together, he thought she'd stay with him."

"And when she left..."

"He spiraled into a dark pit he's never been able to

come out of. Alcohol and drugs. Mostly alcohol. He checked into a psychiatric hospital in Asheville and that's when I went to live with Creed and his parents for about a year. One good thing came from Dad at the hospital. He got off the drugs. Not the alcohol, but he doesn't have the money for the drugs anymore."

"Creed's family has been good to you."

"Yeah. I got to see what a healthy marriage looks like from the inside. They were nothing like my parents. I'm not saying they were perfect or that they didn't disagree occasionally, but it was how they handled the disagreements that was eye-opening. If they argued in front of their family—or me—they later apologized. And they never once hit each other." She smiled, a smile of love that took Dominic's breath away. What would it be like to have that aimed his way?

She looked up. "Anyway, that's the kind of marriage I want, that I'll fight for. That I'll model for any children I might have."

And just like that, he could picture her as a mom. A wife. A—

Dominic shut those thoughts down. He wasn't here to find a wife. He was here to put a killer behind bars. A killer who might very well turn out to be her brother.

Until he knew for sure which way this was all going to play out, distance was important. He took her hand and squeezed her fingers. "If Noah didn't kill Carl, then he's going to be all right because of you."

"He didn't kill Carl," she mumbled, sounding like she might be on the verge of dozing off. He slipped an arm across her shoulders and she settled her head against his chest.

He sighed. *Way to keep your distance, O'Ryan.*

FIFTEEN

Katherine wasn't sure how long she slept, but it had been several hours of much-needed rest. And waking to find her head snuggled up under Dominic's chin wasn't a bad feeling either.

Okay, it was actually pretty glorious.

Until she remembered he wasn't completely convinced Noah hadn't shot his partner. She thought he was leaning in that direction, though. But until the real killer was brought to justice, she wasn't sure he'd come around to fully believing Noah without that.

Even so, she wasn't ready to move from her spot. The fact that he didn't seem put off or repulsed by her dysfunctional family revelations gave her hope. Growing up, there had been many times people had judged her because of her parents and she'd had to refrain many times from shouting, *I'm not like them!* Instead, she'd ducked her head, did her best to stay under the radar and set out to *prove* that she was different.

"Katherine?"

The doctor's low voice pulled her from Dominic's comforting embrace. Dominic's eyes caught hers and the tenderness there nearly took her breath away before he masked it by straightening and giving his attention to the doctor.

She stood. "How is he?"

"Came through like a champ. Minimal damage and very little bleeding. No broken bones, although the bullet chipped one. Got that cleaned up and he should be good as new with time and some physical therapy."

Tears pricked the backs of her eyes. Good as new for a prison cell? No, she had to find a way to keep that from happening. "Thank you," she said, grateful for the steadiness in her voice. "When can I see him?" Being on this side of the situation was weird and she really didn't like it. Part of her knew that she could simply flash her doctor badge and she'd be given access to anywhere she wanted to go, but if Noah was still out, there was no sense in throwing her weight around.

"I'll let you know when he's back in recovery."

"Thanks." She turned to Dominic. "Do you think Pachinko's goons will try to get to Noah here at the hospital?"

"I don't know. It's possible, but he's got guards all over his room and the hallway. No one's getting to him unless they have permission." He paused. "I'd hazard a guess that if they intend to come after him, they'll do it when he leaves the hospital."

"So, those guarding him will keep that in mind and have a plan in place to keep him protected?"

"Of course."

"Of course," she echoed.

"But the truth is, you're the one who's still not safe."

"So, what do we do?"

He rubbed a hand across his chin. "I was thinking

about that, and the best way to protect both of you is to keep you together."

"Where?"

"Well, your place is pretty secure and easy to guard when people aren't sneaking out on purpose."

She grimaced. "True, but I'd be worried about someone deciding that us being in the same place would be to their advantage to take us all out at one time."

A visible shudder rippled through him. "It's definitely something to consider."

"Or…" She bit her lip and frowned.

"Or?"

"It's probably a really bad idea, but what if we set a trap for them?"

His eyes narrowed. "What kind of trap?"

"One that has bait a killer wants."

"I *really* don't like the sound of that."

"I'm not sure I do, either, but I *really* don't like the idea of continuing this game of cat and mouse any longer. I'm ready for these people to be caught and behind bars." She glanced in the direction of the surgical ward. "I'm ready for Noah to be able to quit running." She sighed. "I want a relationship with him, Dominic. I want my little brother back."

"I know," he said, his voice soft. "It looks like you're making good progress with that."

"Yes, and I want it to continue." She leaned a head on his shoulder. "So…"

"So?"

"How do you set a trap to catch a killer?"

"I don't want you in danger."

"I'm not super excited about the idea myself, but if

it will put an end to this madness, then I'm willing to risk it."

He shook his head. "No. We'll get a double." He gave her the once over. "Beth could do it."

"She's a brunette."

"That's why they make wigs." He gave her a gentle smile.

"What about Noah? I haven't seen a cop yet who has his skinny beanpole frame. He used to be slightly overweight."

"I noticed he lost some weight while he was with us. He was very stressed out."

"But not *strung* out, right? No drugs that you know of?"

"No, he's not an addict. Never touched alcohol, either."

"I should hope not. He's not legal yet." She groaned as the last word left her mouth. "He was stealing cars and I'm worried about underage drinking."

"No alcohol." Dominic sighed. "He doesn't make a very good criminal," he said, his voice low.

"Well, if needing to eat better is the only thing he has to worry about, I'll take it." And she vowed to make sure he was getting proper nutrition when this was all over.

"You're right," Dominic said. "Finding someone to be Noah's look-alike might be a challenge, but I'll figure something out."

Katherine shot another glance toward the recovery room. "I could pull my doctor card and go on back to see him."

"Isn't he still out cold?"

"Probably."

"Then I have a better suggestion."

She lifted a brow at him. "What's that?"

He slid an arm around her shoulders and pulled her back against his chest. "Get some more rest."

"I'm okay. I slept on your shoulder already. It's your turn to sleep."

"I'm too wired. I wouldn't be able to close my eyes. No reason for you not to, though."

"I'm not sure I'd be able to, either." A yawn hit her and he laughed. She rolled her eyes, unable to believe how tired she was. No doubt thanks to the stress of the past few days.

"Even if you can't sleep," he said, "you're safe for the moment. Noah's got several armed guards and while you might not agree with the reason for them, it does mean he's protected."

That was true.

"Ben and Regina are standing guard on this waiting room, so for now…rest."

His soothing tone tempted her eyelids to shut. She kept them open. "I want to check on Creed one more time. He looked like he was in pain. I want to make sure he's got the meds he needs."

"Creed is fine. He texted me a little bit ago."

"Really? So, you guys are big buddies now?"

A chuckle rumbled in chest, sending tingles through her ear and straight to her heart. She liked this. Could get used to it. If he didn't want to put her brother in prison. But for now…

Her lids drifted shut once more.

Dominic knew the moment she fell asleep against him for the second time that day. She pressed a little heavier into him and her breathing evened out. A lump formed in his throat and he had to swallow twice to get rid of it. He could get used to this.

Katherine in his arms.

But…

He sighed. No need to go down that road just yet. He shifted and managed to pull his phone from his pocket. Beth answered on the second ring.

"Katherine and I've been talking," he said.

"Hello to you, too."

"Sorry, how's Noah?"

"Sleeping like a baby. Looks like one, too. If he hadn't shot Carl, I might actually like the kid."

"I'm starting to wonder if he did."

A huffed sigh reached him, but she didn't argue. "What do you need, Dominic?"

"A plan."

She paused. "Okay. A plan for what?"

"It's Katherine's idea. She wants to set a trap to catch the people after her and Noah."

More silence. "I'm listening," she finally said.

For the next thirty minutes, while Katherine slept, he and Beth hatched a plan. In the end, he wasn't completely happy with it, but thought it might have a chance to work. He could only pray it would. "I'll pass this on to Owen when he gets back. He's on the phone down the hall."

"Great. Let us know when Noah's able to be moved."

"Will do." Beth hung up and Dominic clutched his phone, replaying the idea of the trap in his mind.

He still didn't like it, feeling like it left Katherine exposed too long.

She stirred, blinked and lifted her head. "I fell asleep again."

"You did."

"This is getting to be a habit. Please tell me I didn't snore."

"Not even a little. Either time." And it was a habit he could be very happy with.

"Well, that' a relief." She rubbed her eyes, removing any trace of what little makeup she'd had on. The fact that she didn't seem to care intrigued him. "Any word on Noah?"

"I just got off the phone with Beth." He filled her in and then said, "I think everything's in place for your idea. Beth's going to be your double. She's got the ball rolling to get her disguise worked up and delivered."

"Okay. What about Noah?"

"We're bringing in another agent. He's new, but he matches the physical description."

She bit her lip and raked a hand through her hair. "Okay, as long as Noah's safe."

"And you."

"That's a bonus."

He cut her side glance. "More than a bonus. That's a priority. Anyway, we're going to make a subtle, but noticeable production of getting you and Noah home— the agents, not you two. The real you and Noah will be escorted to a hotel room across the street from your place."

Katherine gave a slow nod, her eyes narrowed. He figured she was envisioning how everything would play out. "Two marshals," he said, "one being me and the other Owen—will stay with you and Noah in the room. Two other marshals will stay at your place to give the appearance of guarding it. Beth and the fake Noah will be inside. Creed's going to put Regina and Ben in the area, as well."

"And you think they'll come after us—or rather Beth and the other agent?"

"I have no idea, but if they do, they'll be ready."

Katherine shut her eyes and rubbed her head. "What if another marshal is involved?" she asked, her voice low. "What if Noah's telling the truth and there's some-one who's a mole? Someone you trust because you'd never believe they'd be anything but loyal?"

He shook his head. "I can't even come up with a name for you on that."

She nodded. "I understand, but I think you need to think about it. My vote's on Beth."

He rolled his eyes. "Just because you don't like some-one doesn't make them a killer."

"I know. I'm just being cranky. Forgive me."

"I think you're allowed. And Beth's all right, she's just passionate about her job." He paused. "And I think she was a little in love with Carl. She's grieving like the rest of us, but her grief cuts a little deeper maybe."

"Oh. Well, that explains things a bit. Now I feel sorry for her."

"I know. I do, too."

Katherine frowned. "So, why can she work this case along with other law enforcement, but you can't?"

"Because no one knows if their relationship was any-thing more than professional. To the outside observer, they were simply colleagues who worked well together."

"But you suspect something more?"

"I've wondered, but Carl was surprisingly tight-lipped about the two of them. Said they were friends and he respected her as an agent."

"I see."

"What? There's something behind that *I see*."

"You won't like what I'm thinking. I don't like what I'm thinking."

"Which is?"

She bit her lip, then said, "If Beth and Carl were such good friends—or possibly more—could she be involved in…everything?"

He flinched. He couldn't help it. "No."

"But maybe we need to be very careful and on guard?"

"I… No. She wouldn't."

"I have to admit, I'm concerned."

"She won't be in the hotel room with us."

"But she'll know we're there."

"All right. I'll take steps to ensure that someone has eyes on her at all times. Will that help?"

"Yes. I think."

Owen stepped into the waiting room. "Beth filled me in. Noah's awake and can be moved to the safe house—or hotel in this case."

Dominic turned to Katherine. "Are you ready?"

"Yes, but I want to talk to his doctor, read his chart and make sure I have any medications he might need."

"Of course."

Dominic followed behind Katherine and Owen, his mind reworking the plan yet again while his eyes scanned for threats.

"Marie?" Katherine approached a woman in a white lab coat and Dominic hung back with Owen.

"I have a question for you," Dominic said.

"Sure."

"You weren't too far behind us when we were chasing Noah. Is there any way he could have gotten a weapon?"

"I kind of assumed that he got it from the stolen vehicle."

"I would've thought that, too," Dominic said, "but the owner didn't report any weapons stolen. Said he didn't own any guns and didn't have any in the car. Granted, I realize he could be lying. But his background check came back clean and there's no indication he's lying. So, where did Noah get the gun? More specifically, a high-powered rifle?"

"Beats me, man. As Beth and I both said in our statements, we were twenty minutes behind you. We didn't know what happened until we got the call you were on the way to the hospital."

"Yeah. I know. But I'm starting to believe Noah's an innocent caught up in all of this." He scoffed and shook his head. "I can't believe I said that. He's not innocent as in he's not done anything wrong. But I'm no longer convinced he killed Carl."

"Then who did?"

"If I could answer that, it would make all of our lives easier, wouldn't it?"

SIXTEEN

Katherine ducked into the unmarked SUV and slid into the back seat next to Noah who had his eyes closed, head against the window. She took his hand in hers and checked his pulse.

"I'm not dead yet, sis," he mumbled without opening his eyes.

"Yes, I just determined that."

"What are we doing?"

"Going someplace safe."

Dominic climbed in the front passenger seat and Owen crawled behind the wheel.

"There is no place safe," Noah said. "They're never going to quit coming after me."

"Which is why we're going to stop them."

He frowned at her, but his eyes closed once more, and he slept the short distance to the hotel. Owen pulled around to the back. "We're going in through the kitchen entrance."

"I'll grab the wheelchair." Dominic headed for the trunk while Katherine shook Noah awake.

"Come on, little brother, let's go." He drew in a breath and swiped a hand down his face.

Dominic got him into the wheelchair and Katherine went ahead to hold the entrance door open. She was still concerned about Beth, but right now, she needed to focus on getting her brother into the hotel room. As long as Beth wasn't in the vicinity—and Dominic was nearby—Noah and she were safe.

Owen pulled up the rear then walked past them, key in hand, to an accessible unit. He swung the door open and Dominic pushed Noah inside. It was a small suite with a sitting area, kitchenette and a bedroom with a king bed. The bathroom was large enough to accommodate the wheelchair, but she didn't think Noah would need it.

Once Katherine and Dominic helped Noah into the bed near the bathroom, she grabbed the bag with Noah's medicine and other supplies for keeping the wound clean. She set them on the nightstand and raked a hand over her head.

Noah had already dozed off.

"This is nerve racking," she said, her voice soft.

Dominic took her hand and gave it a light squeeze. "I know."

"I've been in some tight spots before. Rushed to help fallen officers while the bullets were still flying, but this waiting game is almost harder. Scarier. Especially, since I can't help but wonder if Beth isn't involved."

"The longer you have to wait, the more your imagination has time to work."

"That's for sure." But was it really her imagination? She was on edge, waiting for the next shoe to drop.

Dominic walked to the window to look out then paced back to her. "Everyone's in place. They just drove up with Beth and the other agent."

"They'll use a wheelchair, right?"

"Of course. Everything will look legit."

"Good." She ran her palms down her thighs and drew in a breath. "Good."

A buzzing sound reached her, and Owen held up his phone then stepped into the hall and let the door close behind him, leaving her alone with Noah and Dominic.

A shudder shivered up her spine and Dominic must have noticed. He pulled close and she settled her head against his shoulder, feeling his heart thud gently against her cheek. For a moment, he simply held her, then leaned back to cup her chin and tilt her face up to his. "You're an amazing woman, Katherine. I'd like to…"

"What?"

He sighed and closed his eyes. "There's a lot I'd like to say, but now's not the time and I have to keep reminding myself of that."

Katherine couldn't control the sudden uptick in her pulse or the rush of longing his words inspired. "Let's talk later."

"Yes." His gaze dropped to her lips, then swept to Noah, who was still out cold. "Yes, later."

Owen returned, his gaze flicking between her and Dominic. If he thought anything of their closeness, he kept it to himself. "All seems to be fine at the clinic and your home."

"The closed sign is in the window?" she asked.

"Yes, ma'am. With a note saying that if they need immediate help to get in contact with the doctor on call or head to the hospital."

"Excellent. Thank you."

It sounded like they'd thought of everything. Owen

grabbed his bag that he'd set just inside the door and walked to the table, obviously preparing to work. Katherine slid a hand over her hair and longed for life to return to normal. Although, to be honest, if this was what it took to restore her relationship with Noah, then, in the end, assuming they all lived, it would be worth it.

Please, God, let us live.

Dominic's phone rang and he snagged it. "It's Leon."

Owen had just pulled a laptop from his bag. He frowned. "Why don't you take it outside while I call the director and give him a status update?"

Dominic hesitated then swiped the screen to take the call. He opened the door and stepped outside, his voice fading. "I'm just going to check on Noah," Katherine said.

"Good." Owen turned back to his phone and Katherine walked into the room, shutting the door behind her. Only to find Noah sleeping deeply once more.

Maybe she could get some rest, too. The king-size bed would allow her ample room on the other side and she'd be right there should Noah wake up needing something.

But she wanted her phone and had left it in her purse in the sitting area.

She walked to the door and opened it. Owen had his back to her at the table, but his voice filtered to her. "...take care of the kid, but it can't be here. Just do what we planned and it will be fine."

Katherine froze. Had she misunderstood?

Owen turned and caught her watching. His eyes narrowed. "I'll have to call you back."

Her heart thudded. She hadn't misunderstood. It wasn't Beth, it was him.

She stepped back, shut the door and twisted the lock.

She glanced at the nightstand, just realizing the land-line phone had been removed. And her phone was in the den. They'd have to go out the window and around the front to warn Dominic.

Owen knocked. "Katherine? Everything okay? What's going on?"

"Um, yeah, everything's fine. I'll be out in a minute."

"Anything I can do to help?"

"No. It's all good." She hurried to the window and shoved it open. She pushed the screen out and turned to shake Noah's shoulder. "Wake up, Noah. Hurry."

He groaned and blinked up at her. "What?"

"It's Owen."

"What?"

"Get up," she whispered, her tone fierce. "We have to go or we're going to wind up dead." A loud crash against the door nearly sent her into a panic. She shook Noah again. "Get up!"

This time, he seemed to process the urgency in her voice and alarm skittered across his features. "Owen? It's him?"

"Yes. Now come on!"

Another bang against the door. "Katherine, they don't want you. Just the kid. Give him to them and you'll be fine. They'll have no reason to come after you anymore."

Right.

"Noah, *please!*" He pushed himself to his feet, blinked and got his balance. She pointed him in the direction of the window. "Go." Where was Dominic?

A chill skated up her spine. *Why don't you take that outside?*

Had Owen set him up somehow? In an effort to get

her and Noah alone? Noah stumbled to the window and swung one foot over the ledge. Katherine hurried next to him, ready to follow when the bedroom door crashed down and Owen stood there, with his weapon pointed at her. "Don't do it!"

With a grunt, Katherine shoved Noah the rest of the way out of the window and heard him land with a thud and a yelp of pain. She turned back to Owen and rushed him.

Her move took him by surprise, and he jerked. His gun fired, and the bullet zipped past her. She didn't slow her momentum. Instead, she lowered her shoulder and slammed into his midsection. The air whooshed from his lungs and they both went to the floor, the gun tumbling from his hand. Katherine scrambled for it, but a hard hand clamped on her wrist and yanked.

Pain shot through her arm and she gasped, but ignored it, her sole focus the weapon.

A low thud reached her and the grip on her arm loosened, then fell away. She looked up to see Noah holding a lamp and Owen out cold on the floor, blood running from the gash on the back of his head. The air whooshed from her lungs.

"Thank you," she whispered.

"I owed you." Noah grunted and pressed a hand to his shoulder.

Katherine yanked the cord from the lamp and tied Owen's hands behind his back. She wasn't sure how long that would hold him, but the bed was bolted to the floor and she could use that to keep him from running.

She grabbed Owen's cuffs from his belt and clamped one link around his ankle, the other to the wrought iron bed. He could probably get loose eventually, but it would take him a lot of effort and time—and she didn't plan for him to be there that long. She found the handcuff key and pocketed it, then took his gun and shoved it into her waistband.

Once she had him secured, she checked his pulse. Strong and steady. He'd wake with a mighty bad headache, but she was having a hard time feeling sorry for him. She darted for her purse, pulled her phone from it then tossed the device to Noah. He caught it with his good hand. "Call 911 while I check on Dominic."

He dialed and she heard him giving information.

Katherine ran to the door and looked out, but she didn't see Dominic. Without taking her eyes from the area in front of their door, she said, "I'm going to look for him. Will you be okay?"

No answer.

"Noah?" She turned.

He was gone and her phone was on the table. She grabbed it and found her Notes app open with a message from Noah. I'm going with them. If I do, you'll be safe. I'm sorry. I love you.

"No, Noah, no. Noah!" She ran back into the bedroom. The window was still open. She raced to it and climbed out just in time to see Noah open the back door to a silver sedan. "Noah!"

Noah paused, his pained expression searing her and sending fear straight to her heart. He mouthed, "Sorry," got in and shut the door.

The driver looked at her and she met his gaze for a fraction of a second before he peeled away from the curb with a squeal of rubber on asphalt.

Dominic groaned then opened his eyes looking for whatever it was that had hit him. He took inventory and realized he was lying on hard pavement. And everything hurt. Especially his head.

It pounded like he'd run into another tree, all of his healing swept away in less than a moment. What had he done?

For a brief second, panic flared when he drew a blank, but slowly the memories filtered through the haze of pain.

He'd walked out of the hotel room, thinking it would be a good time to do a perimeter check while he explained to Leon that he'd have to call him back, but had rounded the corner of the building and felt a liquid hit him in the face.

He'd dropped like a brick, unable to fight the darkness that had swept over him.

"Dominic!"

Vaguely, he registered someone calling his name. And the sound of sirens? Who'd called?

As more seconds passed, his brain kicked in. "Katherine." His tongue felt too big for his mouth and he swallowed. His throat was as dry as the desert and he'd do just about anything for a sip of water.

He tried to roll and nausea froze him.

"Dominic!" Running footsteps pounded closer. And then Katherine dropped next to him. She cradled his aching head and smoothed the hair back from his forehead. "Dominic, answer me right now."

He cleared his throat. "You're bossy."

A choking sound came from her and she pressed a brief kiss to his lips. The move surprised him. And her, if the look on her face was anything to go by. "Are you okay? What happened?"

"Got sprayed with something. Knocked me out.

Where's Noah and Owen?" He tried to sit up and groaned when the world tilted and the pain in his head spiked. He stilled and waited for everything to settle.

"Owen was the one, Dominic. He's the traitor."

Her words shot straight to his heart and he could only blink up at her. "What?" he finally managed to spit out.

"It's not Beth—it's Owen. I overheard him on the phone with someone and he caught me." She explained about Noah knocking Owen out and then Noah leaving her a note on her phone. He registered the gist of her words, dread and fury mixing together. "But Owen was inside when someone got me."

"He's most likely working with the guy I saw driving the car that Noah got into." She pressed a palm to her forehead. "I recognized the driver, I think, or he reminded me of someone, but I can't place him. Anyway, he and Owen probably arranged for you to come out of the room so he could spray you with whatever it was."

"Wait a minute. You recognized the driver? Who? Someone from the clinic? Was it someone who lives here in town?"

"I don't think so. I'm not sure. It'll come to me. In the meantime, I don't know if anyone else is involved or not, but we've got to find Noah. Again." She gazed hard at him. "You can't trust the people you're working with, Dominic. We have to do this on our own. I don't know how, but Noah's life, and probably yours and mine, depend on it."

He met her gaze. "You trust me?"

She studied him a moment then nodded. "Yes, I do."

He pulled her back to him and kissed her a little more thoroughly compared to the one she'd given him. It was a thank you for her faith in him and, he hoped, a

194 *Mountain Fugitive*

small expression of what he prayed the future held for them. When he pulled back, she smiled, but her eyes were windows to the anxiety and fear rolling within her.

"Okay, let me think," he said. Kissing her hadn't helped the fog in his head, but he forced himself to focus while pushing to his feet with Katherine's help. He stood and swayed for a moment before the ground was solid once more. "Is Owen still in the hotel room?"

"Yes. Unless he woke up and managed to get out of the cuffs."

"Let's go find out."

Together, they hurried back to the hotel room and found Owen awake, hands loose and working to get the cuffs from his ankle. He looked up, his eyes dark, expression fierce. When he saw Dominic, he blinked. "Oh, good, get me out of this. Your girlfriend is in big trouble."

"Actually, you're the one in trouble," Dominic said. "Katherine told me everything. Who else is involved?"

"Are you kidding me? You're going to believe her over me?"

The fact that he did believe Katherine over someone he'd known for a couple of years probably shocked him more than it did Owen—especially after what had happened with his father.

But he did. He never would have thought it of Owen had it been anyone else telling him these things, but this was Katherine. "I believe her. Who did Noah get in the car with?"

"How am I supposed to know? I'm telling you, you've got this all wrong!"

For a split second, Dominic wanted to believe the man, but the murderous look he shot Katherine wiped that feeling out.

Owen must have realized his protests were useless. He gave a low growl and blew a huff of air through his nose. "You do realize you have no proof. Nothing, but her say-so. Who do you think the director is going to believe?"

"I don't know. I'll let him worry about that. For now, I need to know where to find Noah."

The sirens stilled and Creed stepped inside the room. "What's going on?"

"Creed? What are you doing out of the hospital?" Katherine asked. He looked rough but determined.

"My job. Now someone give me a status update, please."

It took all of three minutes to do as he requested and get a BOLO out on the silver sedan Katherine had described.

Dominic sighed. "I've got to call my director and let him know what's going on. We can also pull Beth and the other agent from Katherine's home and let them take Owen in to get this all sorted out."

Owen snorted. "There's nothing to sort out, but if it will speed things along, then fine."

Dominic pulled his phone from his pocket and Katherine gasped. He frowned. "What is it?"

"Let me see the picture on your phone again. The one of the four of you."

"What? Now?"

"Yes, now, please."

He turned the screen for her to see it and she swallowed then met his gaze. "I know who was driving the car that Noah got in."

A bad feeling centered itself in his gut. "Who?"

She pointed to the man on the end. "Him."

SEVENTEEN

"Leon?" Dominic gave a half laugh even as his shock reverberated through the room. He stared at her, his eyes dark with disbelief. Her heart cramped as though in sympathy with every emotion he was feeling at the moment. "No." His low denial didn't surprise her. First Carl, then Owen, now this latest betrayal? It all had to be too much. Maybe more than his mind could handle.

"Dominic—"

"Don't. There has to be a reasonable explanation."

"Of course there may be. I'm just saying that's who he got in the car with after leaving me the message that he was giving himself up to keep them away from me." She showed him the message on her phone.

He shook his head again. "I don't believe it."

Creed's eyes continued to bounce between the two of them and their prisoner who was listening with rapt attention.

Dominic turned to Owen. "What's Leon's involvement in this? If any?"

"Who?" The one-word question was accompanied by a slight smirk, but Katherine wasn't sure if Dominic noticed. The man sighed. "Come on, guys. You can't hold me on her say-so. Let me out of these cuffs and I might not press charges for false imprisonment."

"He's not going to say anything," Katherine said, ignoring him while impatience zipped through her. "We need to be searching for Leon and Noah right now. And *he*—" she gave a pointed look at Owen "—knows how to find him."

Beth stepped into the room. "What's going on?"

Dominic brought her up to speed in record time. Her face paled with each word then her gaze swung to her partner. "Owen?"

Again, he voiced his protests and Dominic eyed her. "Can you do this?"

She swallowed. "You have proof?"

"No proof, Beth," Owen said, "just the sister of a fugitive making her accusations against the marshal holding him. Give me a break."

Beth's gaze swung to Dominic. "You believe her?"

"I do."

Still the marshal hesitated and Katherine gave a frustrated grunt. "Okay, fine. What if I can prove it?"

Owen's eyes narrowed and Dominic raised a brow at her. "How?"

"Give me his phone."

Owen shrugged and Dominic unclipped it from the holder on his belt.

"Not that one," Katherine said, "the one in his back pocket."

This time Owen cursed and tried to get away from Dominic's searching hands. But Dominic finally yanked the second device from the Owen's pocket.

"Use his facial recognition to open it," Katherine said, her voice soft.

Owen glared, his breathing coming faster, raising his chest in agitated pants. "Stop it. This is stupid. Dominic, Beth. You guys know me."

Beth gave him a hard look. "It would answer a lot of questions about some things I've seen and overheard."

"Beth!" Owen's growl echoed through the room.

"You can explain that later," Dominic said to Beth. He held the phone up to Owen's face.

"Look at the last number he dialed," Katherine said.

Dominic did so and closed his eyes. "Leon's." When he opened his eyes, he narrowed them at Owen. "Well? How do you know Leon?"

For a moment the man simply glared. Then his nostrils flared and he drew in a deep breath. "If I explain, I want some kind of deal."

"Only your lawyer can work that out for you. You know that."

"But you can tell them I cooperated. You and I both know that will go a long way toward helping my case."

"Fine. First we need to know where Noah is."

"I don't know where he took him. All I was supposed to do was let the guy know where we were, then try to give him an opening to get you out of the picture so he could grab the kid and his sister."

"So," Dominic said, "I walk out the door and he sprays me with something to knock me out. Why not just shoot me?"

Owen shrugged. "Guns are loud. He was trying to be quiet."

"What?" Katherine asked. "Did he lose the silencer he had when he tried to snatch me from the tubing parking lot? That was him, wasn't it?"

"I have no idea and I don't know what his plan was

once he got his hands on the kid. But, as long as he avoided the cameras and you seeing his face, once he had Noah, he had no issue with you."

Well, that made sense. Katherine rubbed the tight muscles at the base of her neck.

"Who shot Carl?" Dominic asked, his voice low, his body turned as though to shield a blow.

"I don't know. Wasn't me, but if I had to guess, I'd say it was your buddy Leon."

"But you gave him the rifle." Dominic's words were tinged with tightly laced emotion. Katherine couldn't imagine what was going through his head knowing his friend from childhood was a killer in league with a fellow officer who'd turned bad.

"Sorry. He brought his own." Owen sighed. "We were at the warehouse where the drugs were being cut. It was the three of us. Leon, Carl and me. Pachinko pulled Carl into the organization. Carl asked me if I wanted to make some good money at a time when I desperately needed it." He shrugged. "Same with Leon. The high and mighty Mr. Investment Banker skimmed some money from one of his clients and the guy found out. Threatened to go to the cops if he didn't have it back within a certain amount of time. He was panicking and Carl felt him out about how willing he'd be to be involved in drugs. Leon said he didn't care how he got the money as long as he got it and the rest is history."

"And Noah?" Katherine asked, proud of her steady voice. "How deep was he in all of it?"

"Deep enough, but I don't think he initially knew who Pachinko was. It wasn't until he saw the man shoot one of the drug runners that he spooked and realized he'd gotten into something way over his head. Noah ran, told what he knew to the cops and Carl made sure he and Dominic were assigned to keep an eye on him until the trial."

"Only he wasn't supposed to make it to the trial," Katherine said.

"Right." Owen sighed and shook his head. "But I didn't have anything to do with that. Carl set up everything. I'm not taking the fall for his stuff."

Beth gasped and her face paled. Katherine felt sorry for the ones betrayed. And scared to death for Noah.

"Pretty convenient he's not here to defend himself," Katherine muttered.

Owen glared at her.

"So, where would Leon take Noah? Assuming he has him."

"Probably back to the warehouse. Or someplace he thinks is safe." He nodded to his phone. "If I don't check in with him soon, though, he's going to know something's up."

Dominic wrapped his fingers around the device. "Call him and set up a meeting. Tell him to convince Pachinko you want more money. You and I both know he can order it from his jail cell."

Katherine raised a brow at Dominic's demand, but Owen simply nodded. "Sure."

"Don't you mess this up," Dominic said, his voice soft. "You only get one shot at this. If Noah dies, you're going down with Leon and you know that."

"Yeah. I know how it works. I'll do what I can to save my own hide. He can worry about his."

"Nothing like honor among thieves," Creed said.

Dominic dialed the number and held the phone to

Owen's ear. The volume was loud enough to allow Katherine to hear the conversation.

"What?"

"Leon, dude, what'd you hit Dominic with? He's still out cold."

"He'll wake up soon enough. What do you want?"

"You got the kid?"

"I got him. No thanks to you. He said he bashed you in the head and his sister tied you up."

"Obviously, he's lying. Take him to Pachinko's second in command. I'll meet you there."

"Why?"

"I need more money. I didn't sign on for all of this and want to be compensated for it."

Leon laughed. "That's between you two. I've got my own problems to take care of."

"Meet me there, Leon. I need the kid as a bargaining chip. Meet me or I tell Dominic everything I know about you."

Silence.

"Fine." Leon's tight voice conveyed his displeasure. "Be there in two hours."

Click.

For a moment, no one moved. Katherine caught a glimpse of the agony in Dominic's eyes before he shuttered them and nodded to Beth. "Get him to the director. I'm going after Leon."

Beth frowned. "You can't do this on your own."

"I'm not going to be alone. I'm going to call in reinforcements on my way."

"You'll tell them I cooperated, right?" Owen asked.

Dominic grunted. "I'll tell them."

Creed looked at Katherine. "You need to go on home.

Once Noah's back in custody, Dominic will let you know." He looked at the Dominic. "Right?"

"You'll be the first person I call."

"No," she said, "I want to be there when they find Noah."

"There's nothing you can do, Katherine. This is Dominic's and the other marshals' territory. I know it'll be hard for you to sit and wait, but you've got to let them do their job."

Katherine sighed, struggled to find a good argument that would convince them to let her go with them. "What if something goes wrong and someone needs medical attention?"

Creed shook his head. "If something goes wrong, a doctor isn't going to make a difference."

Dominic thought that statement was a little harsh. Probably accurate, but still harsh. Katherine's flinch said she thought the same, but she finally nodded. "Fine. I'll be at home."

"I'll walk you over there." His head had started pounding again, but there was nothing to be done about it for now. He was going to take care of this himself.

"I'll be fine," she said. "You need to get going. It's an hour's drive and I know you need to get set up."

True. He glanced at Creed. "Are you going with me or staying here?"

"That's not my jurisdiction. I'll let you guys take care of it. Be safe." He followed Beth and Owen out of the room, leaving Dominic alone with Katherine.

He walked over and pulled her into a tight hug. She buried her face into his chest and his heart squeezed with the emotions he'd come to feel for her over the past few days. "When this is all over, can we talk?"

"We can talk." He lifted her chin and kissed her, deciding he could get used to doing that on a daily basis. When he leaned back, her eyes opened and met his. The worry there pierced him. "Please bring Noah back in one piece," she whispered. "Take care of him."

"I'll do my best." He stroked a thumb down her soft cheek. "I promise—I'll do everything I can to make sure he comes back to you."

"Thank you."

"Now, let's get you home so we can get this over with."

In spite of her protests that he needed to get going, Dominic escorted her out of the hotel room. Halfway across the street, Buddy joined them. He followed them inside and went to his food bowl. The undercover agent who'd been masquerading as Noah was still there. He waved at them from the den. "I'm going to hang out here to make sure you're safe."

"Perfect," Dominic said.

Katherine grimaced. "I'll probably pace until you call."

"I understand." He kissed her forehead then went to kneel before Buddy. "You take care of her, too, huh?"

The dog swiped his tongue over Dominic's fingers as though to promise he would be there for her. He had to admit it comforted him somewhat. He stood and turned back to Katherine. She pressed some ibuprofen into his hand and he smiled. "Thanks."

"Be careful."

"Of course. Now I'm out of here. I'll see you soon."

She bit her lip and he forced himself to walk to the door. With one last glance, he twisted the knob and stepped outside. As he headed down the steps, he focused his mind on what he needed to do before he confronted Leon. He pulled his phone from the clip on his belt and dialed his director's number. From the time it took him to get in his car and start driving toward the interstate, they had a plan.

EIGHTEEN

Katherine sat on the couch with Buddy at her feet and the Noah imposter across from her. She'd since learned his name was Mario and that he wasn't a big talker. But he paid attention to the surroundings and walked the perimeter of the building every so often.

Katherine had already almost paced a hole in the hardwoods and decided working on patient files and answering emails would be a better use of her time. Only, she kept finding herself staring at the picture on the mantel of her and Noah. They'd been at the lake and, at the age of sixteen, Noah had been all about selfies. They'd stood at the edge of the water and he'd snapped the shot.

It was her favorite picture of them, but she'd love to have more opportunities for more photos. Funny, Dominic had looked at the picture and hadn't recognized Noah. She could understand that. He looked completely different these days. Harder, leaner...sadder.

Buddy lifted his head and his ears pricked. His head swiveled toward the door and the fur on his neck bristled. Katherine frowned and placed a hand on his head. "It's okay, Buddy. It's probably just Mario." He left about five minutes ago to check the outside. She rose and walked toward the door. Buddy padded along behind her. Just as she stepped inside the kitchen, a hard thud sounded, the door swung inward and bounced off the cabinet nearest it. A man stood there with a gun aimed at her face.

She gaped. "Leon?"

"I knew you saw me in the car." Katherine backed up and Buddy growled then barked. Leon pointed the weapon at the dog. "Call him off or I'll shoot him now."

"Buddy, sit!"

Buddy sat, his body quivering, his gaze on the intruder. The gun swung back to her. "Let's go."

"Where's Mario? What'd you do to him?"

"He'll wake up with a headache, but he never saw my face or what hit him, so he'll be fine. Now, go!"

What was he doing here? He must have suspected something was up—or Owen had said something that tipped him off—and he'd sent Dominic and the others on a wild-angoose chase. Which meant she was on her own unless she could somehow alert Creed.

"Not here. Too many ears to hear the gunshot."

"I'm not going anywhere."

"Noah's depending on your cooperation."

She scoffed, her heart aching. "Oh, please, you and I both know you've already killed him."

His eyes narrowed. "No, I've kept him alive up to this point. As soon as you saw me in the car, I knew I might need him to get to you. He's in the trunk of my car and while as much I hate it, he does have to die. Your actions will determine how fast or how slow that happens."

Katherine stilled. She didn't know whether to believe him or not.

He pulled his phone from his pocket with his free hand and Buddy shifted, every muscle in his body shouting his desire to leap at the man in front of him.

Leon tossed her the phone and she caught it. "The code is all nines. Check the pictures. I even time-stamped them for you. The last one was taken about thirty seconds before I walked in here."

Which meant if Leon was telling her the truth, Noah was somewhere close by. She followed his instructions with shaky fingers and opened the Photos app.

Noah lay in the trunk of a car, duct tape over his mouth, hands bound behind him, eyes wide and staring at the camera. Her heart thudded when she noted those were not the eyes of a dead person. She closed the app and held on to the phone. "You could have taken these and then killed him."

"I could have, but I didn't. I needed insurance."

"So, I just walk out of here and let you kill us both?"

"Like I said, it can be painful or quick."

"I see." *Think, Katherine, think!* He seemed to have forgotten she still had his phone. "Well, uh…we have some time, right? After all, Dominic and the others are headed to Asheville thanks to your shenanigans. Can you at least answer some questions?"

He blinked at her, apparently thrown by her temerity. She pressed her advantage. "Did Noah kill that marshal or did you?"

He stepped toward her and Buddy went into a fit of barking that sent Leon stumbling backward. "Shut him up!" He swung the weapon back toward the dog and Katherine grabbed Buddy's collar.

"Let me put him outside. I'll block the door so he can't get in." She didn't bother to wait for Leon to respond, just guided Buddy to the doggy door and wrestled him out. She shoved the plastic piece over the opening, pressed 911 on the phone and hit Send. When she was sure the volume was down, she stuffed it into the front pocket of her jeans and turned to find the gun trained back on her. "So? Did you kill Carl?"

Leon's frown had deepened. "Carl was an idiot."

"I thought he was your friend."

"He was, but that doesn't make him smart. Do you know he actually suggested we bring Dominic into the organization?"

"Dominic?" She couldn't stop the huff of disbelief that slipped out.

"See? How long have you known him? Not nearly as long as Carl and you see how ridiculous that idea is. Carl's known him for years and he didn't have a clue as to Dominic's goody-goody bent—or if he did, didn't think it would keep him from joining us if the money was right. I tried to tell him, but he said everyone has a price and he was going to feel him out."

"So, you shot him and tried to frame Noah for it."

"If I hadn't missed hitting Dominic, none of this would have been an issue and I would be back in my office and the world would be right again."

Shock and sorrow held Katherine still for a brief moment. "Do you feel nothing? Killing people doesn't bother you?" she asked, keeping her voice low. Buddy had stopped barking and she didn't want him to start up again since it looked like Leon had forgotten about him.

"Of course it does. I regret so many things, but I can *not* spend the rest of my life in prison. I was born for greater things and prison is not in my future. I only needed the money to invest in a sure deal. I planned to put it back as soon as I could."

"Only that sure deal fell through and you became desperate."

"Yes." His jaw tightened farther, and his eyes flashed while the gun lowered a fraction.

Katherine grabbed the kettle from her stove and threw it at him. He gave an enraged scream when the kettle slammed into his arm. He dropped the gun and Katherine raced to the back steps that would lead her down to the clinic.

A crash sounded behind her and she spun to see the doggy door on the floor and Buddy flying through the air to clamp his jaws around Leon's forearm. They both crashed to the floor and another scream ripped from the man's throat while his free hand searched for the weapon.

Katherine raced over and grabbed the gun from Leon's reach and turned it on him. "Buddy! Off! Buddy, come!" She wasn't sure what command to use, but he must have understood because he froze then released Leon's arm and padded over to stand next to her. Leon rolled to his knees cradling his bleeding arm.

"You're going to pay for this," he growled even as tears of pain swam in his eyes.

"No, you are." She held the gun on him, her hand steady, grip firm. "Take me to Noah."

"Not a chance. I'll let him die there."

He would, too. "Then tell me where he is and I'll let you go. Give you a head start. Please. I don't care if you get away. I just want my brother safe."

"See, what you don't seem to understand is that as

long as he's alive, Pachinko will never stop looking for him. Just for the sheer revenge of it. He sent me to finish the job and if I don't do that, then he'll come after me, too. And I don't plan to let that happen."

He lunged at her and Buddy went into a frenzy of barking. But Leon's hand clamped around her ankle and yanked. She hit the floor—and the weapon did, too.

Leon's hand clamped around it.

Hearing Buddy's frantic barking, Dominic raced up the steps to Katherine's apartment with Regina and Ben behind him. He found the door kicked in and his heart slammed a hard beat in his chest.

"Katherine!"

"Dominic, help! He's got a gun!"

Katherine and Leon wrestled on the floor, her hands wrapped around the wrist attached to the hand that held the gun. Buddy had his jaws clamped around Leon's calf.

"Leon! Give it up!"

A howl of rage and pain echoed through the kitchen and Dominic leaped forward to stomp on the weapon, pinning it—and Leon's hand—to the hardwood. Regina and Ben had joined in, adding their shouts for Leon to stop fighting.

Buddy seemed to realize Dominic and the others had it under control and backed off to sit next to the plastic doggy-door covering that hadn't been enough to keep him from coming to the rescue.

Dominic grabbed the weapon and Katherine released her grip and rolled to her side, breathing hard. She looked up at him. "We're going to have to talk about your choice of friends."

"Yeah."

Leon had gone still, bleeding all over Katherine's kitchen floor. And weeping. "I'm sorry, Dominic, I'm sorry."

"I heard how sorry you were."

Katherine pulled the phone from her pocket and tossed it to Dominic. He caught it midair and dropped it onto the counter. Leon let out another sob, his shoulders shaking. Katherine stood. "Noah's somewhere nearby. He's locked in the trunk of this guy's car."

Regina nodded. "Mac felt like he was missing out on helping with the case, so Creed let him take that one. They're are combing the streets as we speak."

"He can't be too far from here," Katherine said.

Regina's phone rang and she snagged it. "Creed?" She listened for a brief moment and shot Katherine a smile. "They found him. He's fine other than a ripped stitch or two."

Katherine swayed and gripped the counter. Dominic hurried to pull her into a hug. "He's okay," he said.

She nodded and tears spilled over her lashes. "Thank you for coming to the rescue."

"Creed said your dispatcher called him about a 911 call. He called me and we made a one-eighty to hightail it back here."

"I'm so glad you did."

"Thank you for asking for help."

She laughed, a choked sound, but at least it was a laugh. "I did?"

"Yep, you shouted, *Dominic, help! He's got a gun!*"

"See? I told you I asked for help when I needed it." She buried her face in his chest. "It's all over, right?"

"For the most part. Owen's telling everything he

knows. Leon will, too, given time. We'll get everyone involved over time."

"Good. That's good." She paused and looked up. "I love you, Dominic. I know it might be a little…soon, but I've never…felt this way before and wanted to tell you before…you know…you leave." Heat burned her cheeks, and she ducked her head while Dominic tried to breathe. He must have been silent too long because she cleared her throat. "I've never been one to do things the traditional way, so you don't have to say anything. I just wanted to tell you how I felt." She sucked in a breath. "So if you don't feel the same way—"

"I do."

"What?"

"I do feel the same and was hesitant to say anything in case—" He drew in a ragged breath. "I'm glad you're braver than I am and are willing to speak what's on your heart. I love you, too, Katherine." He paused. "Can we go out on a date?"

She laughed. "Of course."

"Good, because now, we have a lot to talk about."

"I can't wait."

NINETEEN

One month later

When the doorbell rang, Katherine answered it with anticipation humming through her veins. Today was a day for celebration. Noah had testified. Pachinko had been sentenced to life in prison. Two days into his sentence, he'd been killed in the yard, freeing Noah from the worry of constantly looking over his shoulder. True to his word, Dominic had done everything in his power to make sure the charges against Noah were dropped in return for his testimony.

Her brother had been beyond grateful and promised to get his life together. And Katherine had promised to be there to help him do it.

She opened the door and Noah stepped inside to wrap his arms around her in a tight hug. "Guess what?"

"What?" she gasped on a laugh.

"I'm going to college." He shoved a piece of paper at her as Dominic stepped inside to stomp the snow from his boots.

"Congratulations!" She hugged him again and shot

Dominic a grin. She'd never get tired of seeing him at her door.

"Thanks," Noah said. "I'm just going to go sit on the steps and make a phone call. I want to call Mom, and I know Dominic wants to talk to you."

Katherine stilled. "Sure. Okay." As far as she knew Noah hadn't been in touch with their mother and their mother hadn't bothered to inquire into Noah's well-being. The fact that he wanted to call her rankled, but she tried to understand. The woman was his mother. Katherine had called and left her a message begging her to be kind to Noah if he called her. She could only hope she would.

What interested her the most was what Dominic wanted to talk to her about.

Noah walked away and she turned to slip into the arms of the man who'd become so important to her in the last few weeks. "I want to tell him not to bother," she said against Dominic's chest, "but I don't have the heart."

"I know, but it's something he feels he needs to do."

"You've been wonderful with him."

"He's a good kid in spite of his initial not-so-great previous choices and I think his desire to turn his life around is genuine."

"I think so, too."

"So…did you find your father?"

Sadness gripped her, but a sense of hope flooded in, as well. "I did." She'd left early that morning and headed to Asheville with the hope of talking her father into coming back to Timber Creek. His house was waiting for him.

"And?"

"He said he'd think about it." She sighed. "He was such a skilled carpenter that if he wanted to build a business here, I have no doubt he could do it. He just has to want it, though."

"We'll keep praying he comes around."

"Yes."

He gripped her hand. "Can we take a little walk while Noah's on the phone?"

"Of course."

He pulled her into the living area and kissed her. She melted against him and returned the kiss, reveling in the freedom to love him like she did. Now she just had to tell him.

The door opened and Katherine turned to find her brother looking at them with a bemused expression. "Mom said she was proud of me. Dad was at work, but Mom said she'd pass on the good news."

Katherine blinked and breathed a silent prayer of thanks at the supportive words. "Good," she whispered. "I'm so glad."

"Yeah. I am, too. Surprised, but glad." He shot her a narrow-eyed look. "You called her and said something to her, didn't you?"

Katherine raised a brow. "Me?"

He smiled. "I thought so. Thanks."

Buddy whined and nudged in between them. Katherine laughed and scratched his ears.

Noah cleared his throat and grabbed Buddy's leash. "Wanna go for a walk?"

The dog quivered and stood still only long enough to let Noah attach the leash, then he bounded to the door. Noah followed with a wave over his shoulder, then the small apartment was quiet.

She turned back to Dominic. "How are you doing? For real?"

"I'm making it," he said, his voice soft. "Being with you and Noah has lightened my heart considerably. I'm always going to wonder why I didn't see through Carl's facade or notice Leon's desperation, but...I didn't."

"You trusted them because they never gave you a reason not to."

"I know. It's just going to take time."

"Take all the time you need."

He cupped her chin. "I love you, Katherine."

She sucked in a breath and let his words wash over her. "I'll never get tired of hearing you say that."

"I'll never tire of saying it."

She blew out a low breath. "So, where do we go from here? You live in Asheville and my life is here."

"We'll figure it out. It's just an hour's drive right now, so there's no hurry to make a decision on that."

"I guess I could move to Asheville—or at least closer."

He nodded. "We'll see what's out there and if that's something you want to do then we'll make it work."

She hugged him then eyed Buddy's bed in front of the small fireplace. "You do realize that I'm a package deal. And I'm not just talking about Noah."

"I knew that before you did."

Another laugh slipped from her, and he kissed her once more before pulling back. "I want to listen to that laugh for the rest of my life."

A gasp caught in her throat and she stared at him. "Dominic?"

"I want to marry you, Katherine. I don't know when, but soon."

Tears flooded her eyes and she nodded. "Soon."

Joy exploded in his eyes, and he captured her lips to seal the deal.

* * * * *

*If you enjoyed this story, look for these other books
by Lynette Eason from Love Inspired Suspense:*

Peril on the Ranch
Vanished in the Night
Holiday Homecoming Secrets

Dear Reader,

Thank you so much for joining me on the adventures of Katherine and Dominic. I loved returning to Timber Creek, and hope you did, too. You know, Katherine really struggled with believing her brother could be such a horrible person as to shoot a US Marshal in cold blood. She wanted more than anything to believe him innocent—and he was. Of course, sometimes life doesn't work out quite so wonderfully for those of us outside the world of fiction, but regardless, isn't it awesome that we can draw on the same source of strength that my fictional character did? God is ever present, ever loving and ever forgiving. And Dominic...wasn't he a great hero? He believed Noah guilty, but was willing to listen to another opinion. He was open to hearing what Katherine had to say because that's just how he is. I hope you have people like Katherine and Dominic in your life. And I hope you continue to find amazing books to read and lose yourself in the lives of the characters if only for a few hours.

Happy Reading!

Until next time,
Lynette

Get 4 FREE REWARDS!

We'll send you 2 FREE Books plus 2 FREE Mystery Gifts.

Love Inspired Suspense books showcase how courage and optimism unite in stories of faith and love in the face of danger.

FREE Value Over $20

YES! Please send me 2 FREE Love Inspired Suspense novels and my 2 FREE mystery gifts (gifts are worth about $10 retail). After receiving them, if I don't wish to receive any more books, I can return the shipping statement marked "cancel." If I don't cancel, I will receive 6 brand-new novels every month and be billed just $5.24 each for the regular-print edition or $5.99 each for the larger-print edition in the U.S., or $5.74 each for the regular-print edition or $6.24 each for the larger-print edition in Canada. That's a savings of at least 13% off the cover price. It's quite a bargain! Shipping and handling is just 50¢ per book in the U.S. and $1.25 per book in Canada.* I understand that accepting the 2 free books and gifts places me under no obligation to buy anything. I can always return a shipment and cancel at any time. The free books and gifts are mine to keep no matter what I decide.

Choose one: ☐ **Love Inspired Suspense Regular-Print** (153/353 IDN GNWN) ☐ **Love Inspired Suspense Larger-Print** (107/307 IDN GNWN)

Name (please print)

Address   Apt. #

City   State/Province   Zip/Postal Code

Email: Please check this box ☐ if you would like to receive newsletters and promotional emails from Harlequin Enterprises ULC and its affiliates. You can unsubscribe anytime.

Mail to the **Harlequin Reader Service:**
IN U.S.A.: P.O. Box 1341, Buffalo, NY 14240-8531
IN CANADA: P.O. Box 603, Fort Erie, Ontario L2A 5X3

Want to try 2 free books from another series! Call 1-800-873-8635 or visit www.ReaderService.com.

LIS21R2

SPECIAL EXCERPT FROM

LOVE INSPIRED SUSPENSE
INSPIRATIONAL ROMANCE

Witness Robyn Lowry doesn't remember the crime she witnessed—but someone wants her dead. Keeping Robyn alive long enough to testify is US marshal Slade Brooks's hardest mission

Read on for a sneak peek at
Hiding His Holiday Witness *by Laura Scott,*
available November 2021 from Love Inspired Suspense.

Robyn thrashed helplessly in the river current, her body numb from the twin assaults of shock and the ice-cold water.

Gasping for air, she managed to keep her head above the water for several minutes and strained to listen. She'd heard two gunshots moments before Slade had gently pushed her over the ridge, but now there was only the rushing sound of water.

Did that mean they were safe? She had no idea.

And where was Slade? She tried to turn in a circle, but the river was moving too fast for her to take more than a quick sweeping glance around to look for him.

She knew she couldn't stay in the water for much longer. With renewed determination, Robyn angled toward the shore.

Up ahead was a large tree branch hanging over the water. With herculean effort, she reached up and snagged the branch. She used every last bit of strength she possessed to pull herself up and out of the water.

Her feet found the ground, and she emerged from the river to sprawl on the grassy embankment.

"Slade!" Panic clawed up her throat, threatening to strangle her.

She didn't know who she was or who was after her. She couldn't do this alone.

"Robyn!" The sound of her name made her want to weep with relief.

A splash caught her eye, and she saw a dark shadow getting out of the water about twenty yards from where she lay.

"Robyn, I'm so glad I found you. Let's get into the cover of some brush, okay?" Slade's voice was near her ear. "We want to stay hidden from view."

Because of the gunshots.

With Slade's help, she stood, and together they moved away from the river into the wooded area.

"Are you going to start a fire?"

"Not yet. I don't want to draw undue attention if someone is out there looking for us."

"For us? Or me?"

He hesitated, then said, "I'm not leaving you alone, Robyn. We're going to stick together from here on out."

Until when? Her memory had returned? And what if it didn't?

Don't miss
Hiding His Holiday Witness *by Laura Scott,*
available November 2021 wherever
Love Inspired Suspense books and ebooks are sold.

LoveInspired.com

LISEXP1021